MURDER ON THE MIND...

It could hardly be called an act of passion. Or an accident. Or even temporary insanity. The rare poison that killed Roger Harte had been painstakingly prepared and precisely measured. It had taken three long hours to kill him—in the most unpleasant way possible. Inspector Masters knew they were dealing with a very clever character and a cold-blooded case of...

PREMEDICATED MURDER

"A TAUTLY WRITTEN PUZZLER THAT COMBINES THOSE ECCENTRIC BRIT-ISH TWISTS WITH SOME FIRST-RATE SLEUTHING."   —*Dallas Times Herald*

"VERY GOOD."   —*New York Post*

"A WELL-CRAFTED BRITISH MYSTERY."
        —*Publishers Weekly*

D0950302

Murder Ink.® Mysteries

Scene Of The Crime™ Mysteries

(A *Murder* Ink.®*Mystery*)

PREMEDICATED MURDER

Douglas Clark

Published by
Dell Publishing Co., Inc.
1 Dag Hammarskjold Plaza
New York, New York 10017

Dell ® TM 681510, Dell Publishing Co., Inc.

ISBN: 0-440-17044-3

Reprinted by arrangement with Charles Scribner's Sons,
a division of Scribner Book Companies.

Printed in the United States of America
First Dell printing—December 1981

PREMEDICATED MURDER

Chapter I

A perfect June morning. So perfect that even the centre of London seemed to rejoice. All except Detective Inspector Green. He sat gloomily in the big police Rover, noisily sucking a Fisherman's Friend. Brant drove out of the Yard car park and down to Millbank to turn south and west along the river.

Detective Superintendent George Masters sniffed, wrinkled his nose at the smell and pointedly wound down his window. He then turned to Green who, as usual, had made sure of getting the psychologically safe nearside back seat. "You're sucking cough drops. Got a cold?"

Green savoured the lozenge on his tongue. "I think I might be going to get one."

Masters made no comment. He took his large-bowled cadger's pipe from the breast pocket of his grey Windsor check jacket, where it had been kept propped upright by a monogrammed white silk handkerchief. Sergeant Hill, sitting in front beside Brant, turned and said: "It's anti-social sucking winter warmers in a closed car on a hot day."

"Not so anti-social as that gas projector," sluffed Green through a mouthful of saliva and nodding towards the pipe. Masters again said nothing. The brassy box of Warlock Flake with the black sphinx trademark on the lid looked strangely chunky in his slim, well-kept hands. Green disliked those hands: considered them an inbuilt status symbol which proclaimed Masters to be an appreciable number of notches higher up the social scale than most of his colleagues.

Masters rubbed the dark tobacco with the heel of one hand in the palm of the other with great deliberation and gave a few clearance puffs down the stem of the pipe before charging the bowl.

"Hark who's talking," said Hill. "A bloke who smokes the best past of forty Kensitas a day!"

"Stay north of the river, Chief?" asked Brant without turning round.

"For the time being. Cross at Kew and carry on westwards."

"Where to?" asked Green. "Or would that be telling?"

"Not in the least." Masters had now got his pipe going satisfactorily. "We're heading for a place called Lowther Close which is . . ."

"Part of Lowther Turbary," supplied Hill.

"What's the Turbary bit mean?" asked Green.

"Common or green," replied Masters.

Green obviously didn't like the reply. Masters felt pleased that he'd managed to score the small verbal point, but went on to take the sting out of it for the sake of peace. "It was a place where free peat could

be cut in the old days, though I doubt whether any
was ever cut at Lowther."

"All the place is is a village green," said Hill. "Just
past V Division's boundary."

"I'm told it's one of the most lovely villages in the
commuter belt. Tucked away to the south of the river
west of where the old Hurst Park race track used to
be."

"Very exclusive," agreed Hill.

"How do you know so much about it?" asked
Green.

"Because the Metropolitan Police sports ground is
out that way—at Emberbrook. I've wandered about
round there a bit in the past. One Sunday morning, I
went to Lowther Turbary. There was a cricket match
on the green. The pub was open and people were sitting about. Very pleasant."

"What's the beer like?"

"I don't know. I didn't go into the pub."

"Why not? Too toffee-nosed for you?" Green had
finished his lozenge and was now seeking further dis-
traction from the—to him—unpleasant and dangerous
business of road travel.

"I don't know about that. I remember there were
one or two smashers in summer frocks sitting at the
tables with the players who weren't batting. But they
seemed friendly enough."

"So you spent the morning gizzing at bits of capurtle in flouncy dresses. They must have been something to keep you out of the bar. No wonder you
remember it so well."

"Cut it out," growled Masters. "We've got a job to
do there."

They all knew, without being told, that it would be

a murder enquiry. These days all four of them together were rarely detailed for anything less.

"What's up?" asked Green. "Some fat stockbrocker
been clobbered by some underprivileged kid?"

Masters looked across at him, fighting hard to keep
his dislike of the DI out of his voice and from showing
on his features. He had no serious objection to
Green's left-wing political views, but he wished they
did not colour everything the man said and did. Far
to the right, himself, Masters prided himself on taking what he considered a policeman's attitude should
rightly be—impartiality on all counts when dealing
with the public.

"Even you should have some sympathy with this
victim, even though he may have been quite well-off."

Green sucked his teeth. "Oh, yes! Why?"

"He was a war cripple. A man severly injured in
France in forty-four."

Green had served in the army during the war and
had found the life suited him. As a consequence, he
had a soft spot for the old and bold. Masters knew
that the thought of anybody murdering a maimed ex-
serviceman—no matter who he was—would rile Green.

"You mean some yob has coshed a defenceless
man?"

"I didn't say that. He was poisoned."

Green took a battered packet of Kensitas out of his
pocket. "Poison? That doesn't sound like a yob's
work. A woman's trick, more likely. Was he married?"

"Very happily, I understand. No children."

"I still reckon poison's a woman's trick. And it's a
more than fifty-fifty chance that it was a family job.
So if his wife's his only near relative, concentrate on
her."

The car crossed the river and turned towards Richmond Park and Kingston. Masters knew that if he had been asked for a generalisation without knowing more facts he would have given exactly the same opinion as Green. Statistics may be corkscrewed truth, but there are statistical patterns in the incidence of murder, and Green was sufficiently experienced to recognise them.

"His wife had been away all day."

"All the more reason for suspecting her." Dogmatic: no room for argument.

"And he is thought to have ingested the poison in the house of a neighbour. He certainly died there."

"Ingested! What a word to go to bed with!" Green made the comment because he could think of no answer which would support his own assertions.

It was Hill who made the next remark. "So I suppose the neighbour has been asked to explain himself pretty carefully?"

"The locals are keeping him very much in mind," agreed Masters. "But they've got their doubts about him—in both senses—so they've asked us to help."

"Doubts? In both senses?"

"Doubts about whether he's innocent or guilty, and doubts about him as a person. I got the impression that he's a far from popular man in Lowther Close."

"Ah! Neighbours very anti, are they?" Green said it with relish. "Could be an indication that this chap's all right if his snobby neighbours don't like him. I'll bet a pound to a penny he's a chap called Smith—or some such name—who drops his aitches and who's made a bit of brass."

"You could be right. But he's managing director of a cattle food firm."

Green's face fell. "Trust us to get lumbered with a crowd like that. Give me a few honest villains to deal with every time."

"When did he die?" asked Hill.

"Last night. His name was Roger Harte."

"Arsenic? Strychnine?"

"Ricin."

"You what?" Green had obviously never heard of it. "What's ricin when it's at home?"

"When it's at home?" repeated Masters slowly. "Why, it's castor oil."

Green was never at his best when he wasn't sure of his ground, nor indeed when he suspected he was being made a monkey of. "You're pulling my whatsisname. Everybody knows castor oil is poisonous muck, but it's used in every hospital in the world and I've never yet heard of anybody who died from it."

"No?" asked Hill. "They do say that a big enough dose will split you wide open from base to apex and if that's not lethal—and painful—what is?"

Masters wasn't prepared to let the leg-pull go on. In so far as it was possible, he wanted Green's co-operation, not a bloody-minded cipher tied to his tail. "Ricin," he said, "is a poison extracted from castor oil seeds, not castor oil itself."

"Never heard of it."

"Unusual to find a murder case, I grant you. But nevertheless it is one of the really dangerous poisons. I looked it up before we left the Yard. I read that it is so actively toxic that two-thousandths of a milligram is sufficient to kill a rabbit."

Green, at least, was good at sums. "Two-thousandths of a milligram! Suffering catfish! A rabbit weighs what? Two pounds? So it works out at one-thousandth to the pound. A good size chap weighs about a hundred and seventy. So seventeen-hundredths of a milligram would see him off." Green stared at Masters. "Here, wait a minute. An ordinary tablet you take for a headache—like an aspirin—weighs five hundred milligrams. That's over a thousand times as much as it takes of this ricin stuff to make a bloke snuff it."

"Quite right," said Masters soberly. "At least you are quite right if you ignore the fact of interspecific differences."

"Meaning?"

"That all species do not necessarily respond to pharmacologically active agents on an exact *pro rata* basis. So a man may not succumb to an exact weight ratio of poison *vis-à-vis* a rabbit. In other words, it may need correspondingly less, or even more, to kill a man."

Green accepted this and passed straight over to a complaint. "It still means we'll be looking for a dollop of poison no bigger than a pin head, dunnit?"

"We don't have to look for it. It's in Roger Harte's corpse."

"OK. Where it came from, then."

Masters nodded and tamped his pipe. Hill offered Green a cigarette and asked: "What symptoms are there with ricin poisoning? Arching of the body, like when somebody's taken strychnine? Vomiting like with arsenic?"

Masters paused a moment before replying. "*Risus sardonicus*," he said slowly. "That's the term, I think."

"What for? Ricin poisoning?"

"No, strychnine. The grinning expression produced

by spasm of the facial muscles. And the spasm which bends the head and feet back is called . . . come on, somebody. I've forgotten. Give me a clue."

Green, who had the memory of an elephant for things criminal—as opposed to medical—wrinkled his forehead. At length he said: "Never heard of it."

"It doesn't matter."

"If it doesn't matter, what the hell are we bashing our brains about it for?"

"I was wondering how the pathologist came to decide Harte had been poisoned with ricin. Hill's question started me thinking. It's a very obscure poison. Not the sort any doctor can have seen much of."

Green sat back in his corner. "We can ask when we get there. Aye, aye! Kingston. Hotbed of drug taking, this place."

"Not so much now," Hill said. "The local coppers have done a good bit of cleaning up here."

As the car nudged forward round the one way traffic route, Brant said: "I wish they'd do something about this lot. It comes to a standstill as often as not."

The car dwarfted by buses. Five lines of traffic pulling down towards lights, ready to speed off in three directions at the given signal. "Blast! I'm in the wrong lane. I want right here."

Green was getting jumpy. A Green Line bus engine was panting noisily a foot or two behind his head; a double-decker literally blotted out his window; and immediately in front the diagonal red and green stripes on the back of a thirty tonner shimmered with the throb of the bodywork.

"Go with your own line," commanded Masters. "Don't attempt to move to the right. Straight ahead, and then sort yourself out later." It was said out of kindness to Green whose knuckles showed white on the hand with which he gripped the back of Hill's seat.

The traffic moved forward ten, perhaps twenty, yards and then stopped. "It must be clotted along the road leading to the bridge," said Hill. "They're not clearing the sections in between the lights before they change. Why the hell don't they shut them off and use traffic cops?"

"Just take it easy," said Masters, "and give the DI one of your cigarettes. Light it for him."

"*Opisthotonos*," said Brant.

"Have you gone off your trolley?" demanded Hill. "Not that this little lot isn't enough to send anybody bonkers." He handed Green the cigarette. "But there's no need for you to go inventing new swear words."

"Contraction of both front and back muscles," said Masters, talking in an effort to get Green's mind off the traffic.

"Both?"

"Yes. But the back muscles are much more powerful than the ventral ones. So the back ones actually stretch the front ones till the body arches so much it rests on the back of the head and the backs of the heels. I once heard a doctor say that if a body with strychnine poisoning could be left lying perfectly still and quiet, in the dark, it might not arch at all. But so tightly is it balanced that the slightest twitch caused by noise or light would cause it to leap into *opisthotonos* like a released spring."

"Very painful," said Hill.

"No doubt. Right, Brant, we're away. Straight on and find a quiet side road to bring us back on route."

Green started to relax, and by the time they were approaching Lowther Turbary less than half an hour later, he was almost back to being as normal as he ever could be in a car. He was sucking another Fisherman's Friend as the car nudged into the road which enclosed the main green and fronted the building overlooking it.

"Midday," said Masters. "Too early for lunch yet."

"Hot enough for a drink though," said Hill. "There's the pub I told you about."

"The Gleaner. Nice name. Nice-looking hostelry. Keep going, Brant. The Close should turn off here somewhere."

The houses were not old. No beams, wattle or daub. Just 'turn-of-the-century' substantial dwellings intermingled with short rows each of two or three small cottages. These, however, were no longer the mean homes of labouring men. The bow windows set in place of the former sashes, the new smooth-panelled doors, the wrought-iron knockers and carriage lights, the high standard of paintwork and the hand-carved name boards proclaimed that these were the spots where young executives and their dolly wives had lighted—with the help of guaranteed 100 per cent mortgages from their firms. Ideal spots to light. Hubby could play cricket on the green in the summer. Dolly could cool the undercart of the poodle on the same ground in winter.

"Left here."

Lowther Close was built in the shape of a tennis racket, with the handle touching the green. The houses—all twenty-eight of them—were built in pairs, with those flanking the communal garden in the strings of the racket being, or so Masters supposed, the most desirable. Not that anybody would sneer at any of them. If not exactly opulent, they had all the external signs of belonging to owners of sufficient substance to be cushioned against the effect of a penny rise in the price of bread.

"There's a police car at the top," observed Hill.

As they dismounted, Green said: "It's daft. Look at those numbers, reading from left to right—twenty-five, twenty-seven, twenty-eight, twenty- six."

"Perfectly logical," said Masters. "The Close is numbered quite logically. Odd on the left, even on the right, starting at the green end. When they meet, you get twenty-seven and twenty-eight side by side looking down the road."

"And twenty-eight's our one," said Hill, pointing to a constable coming through the front door.

"No gawping crowd," said Brant.

"Too genteel by half to do that," muttered Green. "In pads like these all you do's gizz from behind the curtains."

It was a pleasant house, judging from the exterior. As they were ushered in by the constable, Masters knew that feeling of welcome which prevades houses solidly built, solidly respectable and solidly furnished. The hall was square and sunlit. The parquet gleamed and the skin rugs looked whiter than a detergent ad.

"DI Dick Woodside," announced a burly man in civilian clothes standing in the doorway of the room to the right of the front door. "I saw you draw up and sent Constable Neave to let you in."

The words were addressed to all four of them equally. It was Green who cocked a thumb in the direction of Masters and said: "Tell him, son. He wears the collar an' tie round here."

"You're Superintendent Masters, sir?"

"Yes. DI Green, Sergeants Hill and Brant."

"We've set up a temporary HQ in here, sir. Not an Incidents Room. It's the late Mr Harte's study or den or whatever he called it. There's a desk, chairs and a phone."

"Very nice, too." Masters wandered in and looked about him. "A sporting man, our Mr Harte, I see. Cricket and tennis."

"Those pictures are pretty old, sir, as you can see. Mr Harte hadn't played any games since the war."

"He was a cripple, I understand."

"Bad case, sir. All down his left side. Head scarred, shoulder lop-sided, arm useless, hip crooked and leg permanently in an iron brace. Couldn't use a stick or a crutch either, because he'd have wanted to use the arm on the same side as the bad leg and that was beyond him."

"It says here," said Green, tapping a group photograph of a cricket team, "that he got a blue at Cambridge."

"Double Blue, Mr Green. Cricket and tennis. But in these last years he'd had to content himself with being a non-playing member of the local clubs. He was still mighty interested. Secretary of both right up to yesterday. Died in harness, you might say."

Masters selected the larger of the two leather armchairs and sat down. "Well-known man, was he?"

"And well-liked, sir. Never known such a popular man."

"Pal of yours?" asked Green, exploring a gap in his teeth with his tongue.

"I knew him. Yes." The tone was defensive.

"How?"

"What do you mean, how?"

"Did you get invites for dinner or did you just touch your forelock when you saw him?"

Woodside reddened. "We got on. In pub and club and—though not invited to dinner—my wife and I were here several times on Sunday mornings for sherry."

Masters said: "So he was a popular, friendly man. Was he rich and generous?"

"Not rich, exactly, but he was a consultant engineer and electronics expert. Boss of his firm. Harte, Belov and Company. You must have heard of them."

"Not that I can recall."

"He couldn't have been much of an engineer," said Green. "Not with a busted wing. How'd he managed technical drawings and things like that?"

"I imagine," replied Woodside, "that he was a bit beyond that stage, but it wouldn't have worried him too much. He'd have coped."

"How?"

"He managed most things. There's a fully equipped private workshop at the back of the house. Roger Harte could drill, cut, saw, drive screws—anything you like."

"One handed?"

"Wait a moment," said Masters reflectively. "You've rung a bell with me. Wasn't a chap called Roger Harte the president of some society for providing aids for disabled people?"

"That's him. Pop Pop, he used to call himself in those days."

"Sounds like a two stroke motor-bike," said Green.

"P.O.P. was the society. Initials of Provision of

Prosthetics. He added 'president of' in front and got Popop or Pop Pop."

"Prosthesis," said Masters, largely for Green's benefit, "is supplying bodily deficiencies such as artificial limbs, and it includes false teeth and glass eyes." He turned back to Woodside. "I suppose it was his own intense personal interest that made him work for P.O.P.?"

"You mean because he was so disabled himself? Yes, partly that. But he designed several gadgets for them and made the prototypes."

"Hence the workshop?"

"That's right. He was in the middle of his biggest project ever when he died."

"He told you?"

"Not what it was to be. He was a reticent man about his achievements, or even about what he hoped to achieve, but he'd never try to hide the fact that he was beavering away in his workshop. Well, he couldn't, really. He was a bad sleeper, you see, and sometimes he'd be up pretty early, working in his shop. And you know what an electric drill sounds like when it's biting through hard metal. It can be heard for far enough."

"I'll bet the neighbours loved him for that," said Green. "I'm not surprised somebody did him."

"They didn't mind," said Woodside in all seriousness. "They liked him so much as a man that there was never any complaint about the noise. Of course, he was not inconsiderate. When I said he was working pretty early in the workshop, I meant about seven o'clock. Not much before. Most people round here get up soon after that during the week to commute into London."

"You seem to know a great deal about him," said Masters.

"I live round here. It's always been my patch."

"Whereabouts?"

"You know the way you came in to Turbary? From the south? Well, I live on the road that runs out to the north towards the river. I managed to get a bit of land there a few years ago—just big enough to put up one of those new bungalows. Only took about six weeks to erect and it came a lot cheaper than having one built in the traditional way." The words were slightly deprecatory, but the tone held pride. Masters was pleased to hear it. He believed in pride, probably because he himself had more than his fair share of it. He could never regard it as a weakness: only as a spur to greater achievement.

"So you became an intrinsic part of the community. Good for you. See how your first-hand knowledge is helping us now. But to get back to Harte's hobby. I got the impression you had discovered what his latest and biggest project was to have been."

"I found his notes and sketches. He was only trying to make a man-made heart muscle that would beat. 'To mimic nature's own action' is how his notes describe it."

"Quite an undertaking. And you say he had nearly succeeded?"

"No, I didn't say that. Just that he was happy with the progress."

"Can I see his notes?"

"I've put them in the file." Woodside moved to the desk and took out several dog-eared sheets of paper. "It's all Greek to me. He was using an electric effect in an alloy made of nickel and titanium."

"It'll probably be Greek to me, too, but I'd still like to read it." Masters took the papers and began to study them.

"Don't keep it to yourself," said Green truculently. "Let's all hear it."

Masters handed him the drawings, but kept the text. The murdered man had been methodical.

"Object," said Masters aloud. "To perfect a man-made heart muscle that beats and functions naturally."

"He wasn't aiming very high, was he?" sneered Green.

"To *perfect* does sound a bit ambitious."

"He meant to *construct* a prototype," said Woodside. "To *design* a better one than already exists."

"He said to *perfect*," insisted Green. "There's no blinking what he set out to do."

Masters read on—

". . . a mechanical heart that actually mimics nature's own action . . . an artificial model capable of real heart muscle contractions . . ."

"And expansions, presumably," murmured Brant. "One's no good without the other."

"You're off net," said Hill. "It wouldn't expand. It would just return to normal size. What I mean is, it would never grow bigger. All the movement would be one way—contraction. It's like jaws. Most people think both move when they're eating. They don't. Only the bottom one . . ."

"OK," growled Green. "We've had the lecture."

"Materials," said Masters, "could well be the key to the feat . . ."

"How obvious can you get?" asked Green.

Masters ignored the interruption.

". . . Americans are currently testing various

heat-sensitive alloys. Are they close to success? I must assume so."

"I think he only noted that to spur himself on," said Woodside. "He'd want to beat anybody else."

Masters nodded. "The alloy nitanol (nickel and titanium) is so heat-sensitive that an electric current can make it contract abruptly and relax just as readily and quickly when the current is interrupted."

"There you are," said Hill. "Just what I was saying."

"Intention. First, to create a left ventricle by using a plastic chamber to which strips of nitanol will be connected in much the same positions as muscles are attached in nature (see *Anatomic Atlas*). The plastic will be relatively fragile in relation to the alloy. Steps must be taken to ensure that the nitanol will not tear away from the plastic. Suggest that the edges of the chamber will need to be wafered between strips of metal, as well as being adhered in some way (heat/pressure? annealing?? cement, if one is available that will not be rejected by human tissue?) and finally studded through. (Check whether studs can be made of nitanol or, if made of white metal or silver, this will affect reaction to current or cause pressure splits round holes.) "

"He's thorough. I'll say that for him." Brant was a bit of a mechanic himself and so probably appreciated the details more than his colleagues.

"The chamber must be so designed that the entire surface of the plastic reacts to the movement of the metal. Only if this can be achieved will the formation of static pools of blood be avoided and, hence, clot formation prevented. The correct degree of elasticity for the chamber walls is, therefore, vital. There will be problems if there is too much give or too little."

Masters put the sheets down. "What follows is purely a bench diary, noting progress—success and failure—as each occurred."

"It doesn't give us much help with the case," said Hill, "but it gives us an idea of what sort of character this Harte chap was."

"Meticulous, he was," said Green surprisingly. "See these little working drawings? Neat as a new pin and done by a chap with only one hand. He must have been a sticker, that boy."

Masters looked at them. "They certainly suggest that Harte, once he set his mind to anything, went steadily ahead with the project until he'd finished it. A thoughtful man, I'd say. One who planned very thoroughly before making each move."

There was silence for a moment. Masters collected the papers and put them back in the file. "Now, having got some insight into Harte's character, we'd better move on a bit." He addressed Woodside. "Is his wife here?"

"Not here in the house. But she's in the Close, staying with friends. She's badly cut up by all this. More cut up than I'd have thought, really." Woodside said this almost to himself, as an afterthought. But its significance was not lost on Masters.

"Are you implying that she did not care greatly for her husband?"

"Lord, no, sir. Just the contrary. Sarah Harte looked after Roger like—well, almost as if he were her child. She'd had to nearly all their married life. No, she cared all right. But it's her attitude that surprises me. She's a self-possessed woman, is Sarah. Well controlled, you know."

"They're a type," said Green. "The ones of uncertain age who pinch kids' places in supermarket queues. Usually run to puce make-up and push those baskets on wheels like battering rams all over the shop."

Woodside stared at the Yard Man in open distaste. "Sarah Harte is not like that. She knows her own mind and she'll stand up to anybody who's in the wrong, but she wouldn't barge and push. Come to think of it, she wouldn't have to. She's got the sort of presence which opens up avenues in front of her."

Green sniffed in disbelief. Masters asked: "But you're serious when you say she's gone to pieces over her husband's death?"

"Yes, sir. Not completely to pieces, of course. I'd have expected to see grief on her face, but I'd have bet anything you like she'd have remained dry-eyed and upright. I saw her this morning. She's weepy and bowed. Aged, too."

Masters nodded sympathetically. "She was away all yesterday?"

"Shopping in town, and then going on to a meeting of some old girls' association she belonged to. Annual bun-fight. Dinner followed by theatre. That sort of thing. Expected back about half past eleven."

"When did she actually get back?"

"On time. We thought it best to let her come back without knowing her husband had died about an hour and a half before. I arranged with Harriet and Leslie Casper to take her in. They're her closest friends. They live at number nineteen. Though anybody round here would have had her—even next door."

"Where he died, you mean?"

"Number twenty-seven. Name of Rencory. Milton and Maisie."

"You sound as if you weren't one of their greatest admirers."

Woodside wrinkled his nose. "I've never found anything against them I could put my finger on, but . . ."

"Like the rest of the people round here you don't like them?"

Woodside nodded. "Everybody loathes them."

"And yet Roger Harte was visiting them last night."

"I should have said everybody except Harte. He did his damndest to get people to accept them—urged his friends to make allowances and to live amicably."

"Allowances? For what?"

"Rencory's a self-made man. I admire him for that. Trouble is, he never lets anybody forget it—least of all himself. He's a blusterer. No . . . no finesse about him. Maisie's all right. A bit mouse-like, I've always thought."

"You're a snob," accused Green. "You've got yourself dug in here—probably because these people think it smart to have the local DI on their side—and you're swimming with the tide."

Woodside glared at Green for a moment and then took a deliberate step towards him. "You're beginning to try my patience, Mister Green. I don't know what bug is biting you, but whatever it is, find it quick and tread on it, or I'll tread on you. And I'd remind you of one little obscure paragraph in Police Regulations which states that an officer can be sentenced to two years hard for calling into question without justification the professional competence of another officer. Any more from you and I'll invoke that clause as well as performing a bit of cosmetic surgery on your ugly mug."

Green didn't flinch. He stared straight back. "Try it, son. Either or both, and you'll think it's your birthday."

But Woodside was not easily intimidated, either. "Go ahead if you think I'm joking."

What else he was about to add was not heard because Masters stepped in. "Cut it out, both of you. This isn't a playground."

"It has been suggested, sir, that I'm not taking an impartial view of this case and that I am biased against Rencory."

"I know. But you must forgive Mr Green. We all have our methods. He has years of success behind him based solely on gaining information from people stung into replying unwisely to his particular brand of abrasiveness. That aside, are you?"

"Am I what, sir?"

"Biased against Rencory."

"I think not, sir, in so far I've not arrested him nor invited him to the station to help in our enquiries—which I could very well justify as it appears Harte must have ingested the poison on his premises."

"Not an answer, Mr Woodside. I suggest you were so well aware of your dislike and mistrust of Rencory that you asked for our help."

"True—up to a point, sir. My real reason for asking for you is that I have been so personally involved with these people that I might make a bad job of the investigation. My attitude must already be coloured to some degree—and you can't prejudge in a murder case."

"Fair enough. Harte, Mrs Harte, Rencory. You've

dealt with those. Now what about the death itself and
medical reports?"

Woodside shrugged. "We've got very little. Harte
went into Rencory's house at about seven o'clock last
night . . ."

"Invited or uninvited?" asked Green.

"Rencory says uninvited, and I've no reason to disbelieve him, because that was Harte's way. He'd drop
in anywhere at any time."

"On what pretext last night?" asked Masters.

"Rencory said he didn't give one. Just said that his
wife was in town on some hen party and he was
feeling lonely so he dropped in . . ."

"It stinks," said Green. "If Harte was nosey-botty
with every other person in this Close and was feeling
lonely, why should he drop in on Rencory?"

"That's a point," admitted Woodside. "But according to Rencory, and vouched for by his wife,
Harte just turned up. The Rencorys were about to
have coffee after an early supper, and invited Harte
to join them, which he did."

"Had he eaten before calling?"

"Yes. His wife had left him a variety of tinned
foods unopened. He'd opened and eaten them—
chicken breasts and asparagus tips, actually. He died
about three hours after arriving at the Rencorys."

"Did a doctor get there before he died?"

"Yes. Doctor Stewart lives in the Turbary. Rencory
called him some minutes before nine. As soon as he
saw Harte was feeling dickey, was how he put it."

Masters stood up. "It's one o'clock. Can we get
some lunch at your pub?"

"The Gleaner? Yes. Ploughman's or the real thing.
They've a good standard."

"Will you join us?"

"I'd like to, sir. Dr Stewart is likely to be there at this time. He usually drops in for a half after morning rounds."

As they left the room, Green said to Woodside: "We've got some talking to do, lad. For your own good. We'll do it over the drink I'll let you buy me in a minute. And as I've a cold coming on, it might as well be a double scotch."

Chapter II

Dr Stewart was young—no more than thirty-five by Masters' guess—tall, with dark wavy hair, a good-looking face and a nasal voice that suggested that his mother had not succumbed to the fashion—then current—of having his adenoids out when a child.

"We've heard of you," said Stewart who, though a big man, was dwarfed by Masters' size. "But this one is going to be a bit of a teaser, I think, even for an expert like you. Poor old Dick Woodside, who is, I know, a good copper, didn't know where to begin last night. I could see him floundering. It was obvious he scented defeat from the moment he appeared."

"He's too involved personally, perhaps," murmured Masters before tackling the pint of Worthington that had been drawn for him.

"Maybe. I noticed he's hob-nobbing with your inspector. Picking up a few hints, is he?"

Masters looked round. Green and Woodside both had shorts and were in earnest conversation near the window. Green had an unlit cigarette dangling from his lower lip, bouncing up and down as he talked.

"Hints? I think there's a clash of temperament being ironed out in the interests of justice. Now, doctor, I've some questions."

"Fire away."

"Have you ever met a case of ricin poisoning before?"

"No. And I should think very few people have."

"Good. What made you decide that ricin was the toxic agent which killed Harte?"

"I didn't—not categorically, that is. I suggested it as a possibility. The hospital pathologist confirmed it."

"What made you suggest it?"

"In a minor way, we doctors are detectives in our own right. I have a table of poisons, antidotes and treatments. But before you can give an antidote or treatment, you have to identify the poison. It's sometimes easy if there's a bottle of pills or weed-killer near the patient. But when there isn't you have to rely on signs and symptoms together with timings and the like."

"Timings?"

"Some poisons knock people out like a light. Some are delayed action jobs. It's all in the table. Cyanide and cyanide gas, for instance, are rapidly fatal. Barbiturates and aspirin produce a rather lengthy depression, drowsiness and finally coma."

"What does ricin do?"

"Toxic symptoms don't usually come on for a few hours. So after I'd established—from the Rencorys—that Harte had not eaten nor had a drink for at least two hours before he caused concern to his hosts, I felt

I was fairly safe to disregard the more immediate acting poisons."

Masters signalled to the barman for refills, and said: "Please go on, doctor. I'm interested in your technique."

"Having ruled out the fast-acting toxins, I looked for signs of burning or staining of the lips and mouth and found none. So I could then rule out the corrosives. And that's how I went on—eliminating what it couldn't be. Only after that could I use the symptoms as pointers. Some of these overlap, you see, that's why I couldn't be absolutely certain that ricin was the poison Harte had ingested."

"What are the ricin symptoms?"

"At the simplest? You could say that it produces fatal gastroenteritis."

"That's a little too simple."

"First off, as I've already told you, the toxic symptoms do not usually come on for several hours. When they do arrive, they're primarily due to the intensely irritant action of the stuff. So the chap who's taken a dose gets the most frightful diarrhoea with bleeding; an inability to pass water even though the desire to do so is there; and finally, galloping jaundice, due to the liver cells having lost their power of holding back the bile which, as a consequence, diffuses the fluids of the body. The bilirubin index is measurable, as you probably know, and once it gets above fifteen, you've got a case of clinical jaundice on your hands."

"Bilirubin?"

"The principal pigment of bile. Red colour."

"I see. Anything else?"

"Not of importance. I did my check and diagnosis. I tried all the usual treatments—stomach pump, gastric lavage, big drink of salt and water to make him sick, milk to soothe his stomach—everything I could think of."

Masters appeared surprised. "Did Harte co-operate in all this?"

"Amazing, isn't it? A severely maimed man *in extremis,* and yet co-operative! But that was the type of man Roger Harte was. Gutsy. Brave as they come."

"And well-liked, I understand."

"That's the understatement of the year. He was loved by everybody round here. Remarkable! A man with every physical drawback imaginable. Yet he was a leader of men—a sort of proconsul I suppose you'd call him. He moulded opinion by example and force of character. He never raised his voice, he couldn't hurry, and yet he had authority. It wouldn't be too trite to say we shall never see his like again, because I honestly believe we won't."

"Somebody disliked him enough to murder him."

"Inexplicable."

"Did he say anything at all while you were treating him?"

"He mentioned two names. Those of Rencory and his own wife."

"Nothing more?"

"He was in a pretty bad way."

"I see. You were going to tell me earlier why you included ricin in your list of possible toxins."

"I nearly didn't include it. I was a bit worried about the shortness of the time it had taken the poison to start acting. I was working, you see, from a datum point of seven o'clock—which was the time he had drunk the coffee, and I didn't think there'd been time enough since then in which to contract jaundice.

But it suddenly occurred to me that I couldn't be sure that he had taken the poison in the coffee. I'd automatically asumed that it had been ingested with the last food or drink he'd taken. Then it struck me that he could have taken it, perhaps, with the last meal he'd had in his own home.''

"Wise of you—even though Woodside wouldn't agree that he took the ricin in his own home."

"In very few cases like that are the symptoms so clear cut that you can positively identify the one poison which could have caused the trouble. So many of them cause sweating, for instance, so many sickness, so many a coma . . . you just have to play the permutations and combinations in the absence of the one proof you really need—the empty container. So I put down four possibilities for the pathologist to consider."

"He tested the stomach contents for ricin?"

"He would, of course. But I suspect he got his information from an examination of the liver."

Masters finished his drink. "Are you free to join us for lunch?"

"I'd like to, but I have a clinic this afternoon—all the dollies who are infantising."

"In that case, could I ask you this one last question? Where would anybody obtain ricin?"

The doctor shook his head. "Nowhere that I know of."

"It's not produced for any medical purpose?"

"I've never heard of one."

"Thank you, doctor."

"That the lot?"

"Unless you care to give me your opinion of the relationship existing between Harte and Rencory who is, I understand, cordially disliked by everybody in Low-ther Turbary—particularly in the Close."

Stewart grimaced. "Rencory is not my patient, so I'm breaking no oath of secrecy in telling you that I, like everybody else round here, find Rencory to be a man in whose company I'd rather not be."

"Harte called on him."

"Roger disliked him too, of that I'm sure, and yet he spent his time asking the rest of us to accept Rencory and give him a chance to live amicably among us. He showed the way by making a point of calling on Rencory and of inviting him to our local functions. That shows you the type of chap Roger was."

"Was Rencory grateful? Or was he resentful of Harte's efforts on his behalf, would you say?"

Stewart grinned. "You're an artful devil. You want me to say Rencory was resentful—because he was in Harte's debt for the kindness shown."

Masters shrugged his shoulders. "It *is* a possibility, you must admit. And as Harte only spoke twice in your presence—once to name his wife of whom, pre-sumably, he was fond . . ."

"Wrapped up in Sal—Sarah."

". . . and once to name Rencory, it could have meant that he was trying to tell you who his mur-derer was."

Stewart was silent for a moment. Then—

"Read into it what you like. It sounds logical—for a dying man to call on the woman he loved and to name his killer. But I didn't hear it like that. And for my money, Rencory was duly grateful to Roger."

"I'll take your word for it."

"Please do, because I cannot testify otherwise. In his agony—and he was in agony—he called his wife's name. There was no bitterness, no accusation in his tone when he mentioned Rencory. If anything, the reverse."

"How the reverse? Forgiving, perhaps?"

Stewart set his glass down. "God, you people!"

"I've upset you," said Masters soothingly. Then his voice changed. "Or have I struck a chord?"

"Yes, damn you, you have. Forgiving is exactly the word I would use to describe the way he said the name, looked at the man, and raised his arm towards him. Forgiving! And I suppose in your book forgiving is condemnation."

"Not necessarily," murmured Masters. "But you must agree I wouldn't be doing my job if I didn't consider all possibilities."

"It's not that I object to. It's the way you wormed it out of me and then twisted it—viciously—before I saw what was happening."

Masters grinned. "Don't be so despondent. At the moment I don't see how Harte could have known that Rencory administered the poison—unless he injected it, and that would have had to be done by force."

"I wish to heaven he had injected him."

"Oh, why?"

"Because one of the peculiarly interesting things about ricin is that when injected—in small doses, that is—the body produces an antitoxin precisely analogous to those produced against bacteria."

"And so it isn't toxic?"

"Not in doses as small as those that kill if taken by mouth."

They stood silent for a moment, then Masters asked: "Why was it Harte could do no more than say a couple of names and lift an arm? What I mean is, if he could do those things, why couldn't he have said more, done more?"

"Ricin has a direct action upon the medulla oblongata, which is the most primitive part of the brain, and situated low down at the back of the head. The medulla controls all the vegetative functions of the body . . ."

"Vegetative?"

"Those not under the controll of the will. The ones we do automatically, like breathing, digesting food and so on. Consequently, Harte's respiration was affected seriously and there was a great fall in blood pressure."

"So though the will to talk and gesticulate was unimpaired, the body itself was incapable of obeying the brain through sheer weakness?"

"In lay terms, yes. He couldn't breathe, his heart had nearly stopped and he had diarrhoea and galloping jaundice. You don't get soliloquies and grandiloquent gestures in such circumstances."

"I can appreciate that, and I know how you must be feeling over the death of your friend and patient. Thank you for talking to me. You have helped tremendously."

"Any time," murmured Stewart, less than graciously, as he moved to the door.

"The barman," said Hill, as they took their seats at the table, "was telling us a story about this chap Rencory."

"What was it?"

"One morning, only a few weeks ago . . ."

"Just a moment," said Masters. "Mr Woodside, we

know Rencory is a self-made man. What did he make himself out of? Cattle cake?"

"That's it. Cattle food. Pig nuts and feed cake. That sort of thing. He has a new factory—not a big one—about four miles out."

"And before that?"

"He'd got an old mill somewhere in the East End, near the docks."

"And when did he come to Lowther Turbary?"

"Just before last Christmas. Soon after he got the new factory. He'd lived in London—handy for this old place before then."

"I see." Masters turned to the waiter who had approached. "Ham salad to begin with. Cheese and coffee to follow."

When their orders had been taken, Hill began again. "A few weeks ago, on a Saturday morning, Roger Harte had a postcard delivered to his house, number twenty-eight, from a debt collecting agency called Regane . . ."

"Conscious humour among the bulls! Sorry, Hill, go on."

"The card said that Rencory owed Brodies, the department store, well over a hundred quid which he hadn't paid."

"Despite, I suppose, repeated requests for settlement?"

"That's the idea, Chief."

"So Brodies had handed it over to this Regane firm to collect."

"Bang on again, Chief."

"But they'd got the address wrong. They'd sent it over to Harte's number—accidently on purpose. An old trick."

Hill nodded. "The point is, Rencory didn't owe any money."

"The devil he didn't!"

"Not a bean. He created hell with Brodies who swore they'd never given any debt-collecting firm his name . . ."

"And I suppose when Rencory tried to trace Regane and Company Limited, he found there was no such firm."

"How did you guess, Chief?"

Masters leaned aside to let the waiter put his plate down. "It seemed obvious. And it's very nasty. These debt collectors often send postcards to neighbours' addresses to try to shame the debtor into paying. But in a place like Lowther Turbary, the postman would read the name rather the number. So how did the posty come to give Harte a card addressed by name to Rencory?"

"I hadn't asked myself that question, Chief."

"You should have done. Pass the mustard, please."

"I suppose the postman was too busy reading the juicy bit on the business side to . . ."

"No." Masters ladled mustard on to the side of his plate. "I'll bet the name was deliberately typed so high up on the card that the franking machine practically obliterated it."

Woodside, who was sitting on Masters' right, said: "You're quite right, sir, it was. I saw it."

"Rencory brought it to you?"

"He demanded our help, but there was nothing we could do about it. The thing was a hoax."

"A pretty dirty one. But we've interrupted Hill's story."

"There's not much more," said Hill who, in spite

of the heat of the day, was tackling a plate of roast lamb. "It appears Harte wanted to keep it quiet, and took it in to Rencory in person . . ."

"Rather than re-address it and then put it in a letter box for another public airing?"

"That's right."

Masters folded a leaf of lettuce preparatory to spearing it with his fork. "But he reckoned without the postman. The story was all round the Close within ten minutes."

Hill shrugged. He'd never found Masters short on imagination, but he felt it was a bit hard to have his chief know every move in a story before it could be recounted.

"Sorry I mentioned it, Chief. I just thought it would illustrate how much the people round here hate Rencory, and what a decent sort of chap Harte appears to have been."

"Don't apologise," said Masters. "You've told us a great deal." He turned to Woodside. "All that Hill just told us is the truth, is it? It hasn't been embroidered over the weeks?"

"Absolutely right," said Woodside. "There was no mention of Rencory's name on the front side of the card to give the game away to the postman so that he would know to put it in number twenty-seven's box despite Harte's house number being on it. But I don't see how that's going to help you discover who killed Harte."

"It isn't," said Green. "It can't. That dirty trick was pulled on Rencory. He was the victim that time."

Masters said nothing. Apart from his own dislike of Green, he couldn't begin to explain the stirrings in his mind. But Brant wasn't prepared to agree that

Masters couldn't wring blood out of a stone—if he said he could. So he chipped in: "Of course it'll help. If only to show us we've got a sadistic maniac to deal with in this neck of the woods."

Green sneered. "You can't say that a chap who writes a hoax postcard is a murderer."

"If he isn't, it means there's more than one criminal lunatic round here. That makes it worse from one point of view, but at least it warns us we've landed in a snake pit."

"Come off it," said Woodside. "We've got as sane and balanced a community in Lowther as there is in this country. Of course there must be some black sheep in the flock, but the crime figures for this area are negligible." He paused for a moment. "Furthermore, most of the crimes committed round here are the work of outsiders—villains who come in on the chance of easy pickings."

Brant wasn't prepared to let it go at that. He said he wasn't talking about theft and such like, but mental instability, and only if Woodside could produce evidence that there weren't as many tranquillisers taken in the environs of Lowther as in any other community of comparable size would he, Brant, accept that this was as sane and balanced a manor as any other.

"Quite right," said Green.

"You've changed your tune," said Woodside.

"No I haven't. All I said was that a chap can't be called a murderer for writing a hoax postcard."

"He that filches my good name, etcetera," murmured Masters.

"I've heard that one, and I'd think a lot more of it if I'd got some cash for somebody to pinch," said

Green, pushing away his coffee cup. He then proceeded to put another cough lozenge in his mouth and to light up a Kensitas to smoke at the same time.

Masters pushed his chair back from the table. He said to Woodside: "Can we stay here tonight?"

Woodside was a bit taken aback. "Stay? But I thought you'd go back . . ."

"What's up?" asked Green. "Can't your division afford the hotel bills?"

"I'll arrange it," said Woodside. "Four rooms?"

"The sar'nts won't mind a twin-bedded," supplied Green graciously.

After Woodside had left to speak to the manager, Hill asked: "Why are we staying, Chief? It's less than twenty miles back to the Yard."

"Because we may have to speak to practically every person that lives in the Turbary and the Close, and as most of them are commuters—the men at any rate—none is available until well into the evening."

"That's a thought," agreed Brant. "They'll be back here by seven o'clock. If we give them time to have a meal . . ."

"An' then talk to 'em in here," interrupted Green. "They'll be round that bar like flies round a cow pat by nine o'clock, fighting their battles over again."

"Battles?"

"Yeah! Golfing battles, rugger battles, stock-exchange battles, big wheeler-dealer battles—the battles of life, son. After that they'll go home an' do battle with their wives for a bit of how's-your-father or because the Sunday joint cost too much or because some correspondent on the telly is too left-wing for their taste. Aggro, mate! Aggro! Life's one long aggro."

Hill grimaced in disgust. "Why you can't just have your bout of 'flu quietly beats me. All we've got to do is solve a nice little case of murder, you have to invest it with . . ."

"With what, lad?"

"Whatever the reverse of philosophy is."

"Try irrational or fatuous," offered Masters.

"I'd prefer imbecility," retorted Hill.

"Watch it!" spluttered Green. "You're getting above yourself, mate."

"Can we go?" asked Masters.

"Where to?"

"Back to Harte's house. As Woodside has set up an Incidents Room of sorts there, we might as well make use of it."

"What about Woodside? Do we want him with us?"

Masters considered the question for a moment. "I think not. As long as he's available should we want to call on him. He can leave the constable who's watching the premises."

"Rightho!" said Green, "I'll tell him to shove off an' attend to his stray dogs."

As they drove the short distance back to number twenty-eight, Masters gave them their instructions.

"I read this as a parochial crime. In other words, I think Harte was killed by somebody here in Lowther. It has all the appearances of a deliberate and successful attempt on the life of an apparently good-hearted, popular man. This increases the scope of our investigations because a popular man is known to everybody or gets about among more people than does an unpopular one. This, in turn, means that many people could be implicated. We must interview—if not them all—at least a fair proportion. We'll cast the net wide. Accordingly, we'll take several houses each."

"For what purpose exactly, Chief?"

"You should know, Hill. You've just heard this area described as a snake pit. We've got to beat the undergrowth and peer in the hedge bottoms to discover the snakes."

"Get to know every bit of gossip we can?"

"As long as there is a factual basis for the gossip, yes. I want to know these people as well as I know the first verse of the national anthem. I suspect they're an anomaly. A sheltered community."

"Hardly that, Chief. They all work in the smoke."

"Maybe they do," said Green. "But when they all get back to their holes at nights and weekends, they close the gates round Lowther and live in splendid isolation among themselves. It wouldn't surprise me if they haven't got knife barriers to block the roads in and out."

The car drew up at the front gate. "Come inside," said Master, "and we'll arrange a suitable division of labours."

Chapter III

Masters felt the greatest reluctance to start his enquiries. The afternoon sun was, by now, beating down, imposing a lethargy unfamiliar to him except—as he well recognised—at times when there were aspects of a case that made him feel as uncomfortable as a member of a concert audience when the singer breaks down. He couldn't put a finger on the cause of his unease, but he'd never believed in the old saw that only the good die before the end of their actuarial span. Experience had taught him that the reverse was so often the case that when he heard of a 'good' man being murdered he immediately began to wonder what the paragon had done to deserve his fate. In other words, he began to consider the possibility that the good man had changed categories somewhere along the line. And this worried him. He had no desire to commit, mentally or overtly, the sort of character assassination that the pursuance of such a theory might lead him to. In spite of the fact that he believed the seeds of murder were, as often as not, sown by the victim.

So it was with some reluctance that he opened the gate of number twenty-six and walked up to the front door. He had reserved this near neighbour—on the other side of Harte's house from the one occupied by Rencory—for himself. He felt the occupants could probably give him a more intimate word picture of the dead man's private life—as seen over the fence—than any of the other inhabitants of the Close. At any rate he hoped so. Because, as he realised only too well, knowing what had killed Harte was not necessarily going to indicate who had killed him, or why.

The door was opened by a woman whom Masters judged, by face and figure, to be on the underside of fifty. She spoke before Masters could open his mouth.

"You're the Scotland Yard detective, aren't you? I saw you arrive before lunch."

"Superintendent Masters, ma'am."

"Goodness! Even I've heard your name, and I don't read the sorbid bits in the papers." Her manufactured curls bounced to emphasise her words and her eyes shone with amusement. Masters decided this one was going to be forthcoming and, fortunately, seemed to have a sense of humour. His instinct told him that this woman was as personable as she now appeared simply because she had married a man with a good enough income to lift financial worry off her shoulders. The same woman, married to a man who earned thirty pounds a week less would, he thought, have a lined face, sallow skin . . .

"You are rather staring at me, you know."

"I beg your pardon, ma'am. A thought had just struck me. I was lost for the moment."

"I suppose you do have a lot on your mind. I'm Jenny Summerbee—just to save you wondering what my name is and being too polite to ask right out."

"Thank you, Mrs Summerbee. Would you mind if I were to come in and ask you a few questions?"

The curls bounced again. "Please do. Eric will be green with envy."

"Eric? Your husband?"

Masters stepped inside. A cool hall, in no way remarkable in size, but giving an air of comfortable living, where people were happy and free to come and go as they pleased.

"My husband. Keen on bringing back hanging and making young men do National Service again and all the other old, square, fuddy-duddy things his sort cling to as the way out of the country's troubles."

"I know. Short hair for lads."

"That's it. He's frightfully inconsequential." She led the way into the sitting room which overlooked the garden at the back. "He says that long hair breeds lice. When I point out to him that girls would still have to keep long hair if the sexes were going to be as differentiated as he wants, he says that lice must be misogynistic because girls don't get them."

"An interesting theory." Masters was still wondering why Eric Summerbee would be green with envy. His wife got back to the subject as she indicated the largest armchair in the room as most suitable to take Masters' bulk.

"He'd want to meet you. And when I tell him you called when he wasn't here . . ."

"There's a possibility I shall see him," said Masters disarmingly.

"Oh? You're going to put everybody in the Close through the third degree?"

She had nice legs. She sat opposite to him and made no bones about showing an expanse of shapely thigh. He appreciated it and then forgot it.

"I should call it *talking* to people."

"Of course. Poor old Roger! Eric is very cut up about him. Everybody is."

"A popular man, Mrs Summerbee?"

She pouted prettily. "Popular sounds too worldly for Roger. Too much like a politician or pop star. I'd say a nice man. Thoroughly nice—always, no matter what happened."

Masters nodded and took out his pipe.

"Do smoke if you want to. I like a man with a pipe."

Masters wondered whether Eric ever obliged her with a few clouds of Balkan Sobranie aroma, and what she would think of his strong Warlock Flake. He began to rub a bowlful.

"Tell me about Mr Harte, please."

"What about him?"

"Health, wealth, activities. His relations with his wife. Quirks, foibles. Anything and everything."

She drew a deep breath. He got the impression she regarded it as a tall order but that she'd have a go—which was exactly what he wanted.

"Well now, as for his health, he was badly crippled."

"I had heard that. Do you know how he came to be disabled?"

"No. Neither he nor Sally would ever say—except that it happened in the war."

"Apart from that, he was as healthy as one could expect?"

"I'd have said so—until last Saturday morning."

"Oh? Did something happen then?"

"We were still in bed, Eric and I. Our bedroom is over this room." She stood up and moved to the open french window. "If you come over here you'll see that we are really very close to the Harte's house."

Masters did as he was asked, and stood beside her. She pointed to a brick-built lean-to behind twenty-eight. "That was Roger's workshop."

"I'd heard he had one."

"You see how close it is to us, and its door is at this end."

Masters nodded.

They returned to their seats. "Naturally, in weather like this, we sleep with our windows wide open. So, in reality, we are not much more than thirty feet from the workshop door."

Masters nodded again.

"I'm telling you this in case you think we were eavesdropping last Saturday morning."

Masters denied that any such idea would ever enter his head.

"Well, as I said, it was last Saturday morning. I was awakened by somebody going into the workshop and moving about—just little sounds. And then, suddenly, there was a hideous noise."

"What sort of a noise, Mrs Summerbee?"

"The high-pitched scream of a powerful electric drill biting its way through hard metal. Eric woke up with a start and swore."

"What then?"

"He got out of bed and went to the window. I think he was going to shout down to Roger."

"But something stopped him?"

"Sally Harte appeared. She'd been dragged out of bed by the noise, too. Eric signalled me to come and look. She was in a pink negligee and mules, with her hair all over the place."

"She stopped her husband?"

"She had to scream to make herself heard. Then the drill was switched off and we heard Roger say: 'Good morning, Sally, what are you doing down here in your dishabille? The neighbours will get an eyeful if you stand up-sun of them in that get-up.' "

"What happened then?"

"Eric and I were laughing, but if either of them had looked up they might have seen us, so we got back into bed."

"Pity. You didn't see much more."

"But we heard. Sally told Roger he was looking tired and hot and asked him if he realised the time was only seven o'clock."

"What did he answer?"

"He was always pulling her leg. He asked her if the sun had wakened her up. Poor Sal! 'Sun?' she asked. 'Nobody for half a mile around could sleep with that racket going on. It really is too bad of you to make a noise like that so early on a Saturday morning.' Eric and I were killing ourselves with laughing. She sounded so cross, but Roger just said something like. 'Nonsense, poppet. They should all be up and about on a day like this. Sluggards, lying in bed, missing the top of the morning.' "

Masters had no way of knowing whether Mrs Summerbee was giving him a faithful report or not, but it sounded authentic to him. And as he reckoned his ear to be as well attuned as anybody's to picking out that which rang hollow in a narrative, he accepted—for the moment—what she was saying without reservation.

"He was a bit hearty? I mean, had he been a fit man, would he have done press-ups first thing every day?"

"He was certainly an accomplished athlete in his day. You probably saw proof of that in his study."

Masters nodded.

Mrs Summerbee went on: "Sal replied that everybody who lives round here is up early enough every other morning to get to business and that Saturday is their day of rest. Roger merely said that he went to business, too, and he was up."

"That sounds just a bit selfish, I'd have thought," said Masters. "Particularly coming from a man whom everybody I've spoken to considered to be most kind and thoughtful."

"Not really. He was fooling about with Sal, you know. Joshing her would be the old-fashioned word for it, I think."

"But yet you heard something of a serious nature?"

"Not serious, exactly. I merely said I overheard something which seemed to show he wasn't perhaps as fit as he might have been."

"I see. What was it?"

"After Roger said he went to business, too, Sal said: 'I know you do, and you shouldn't be up. It worries me. You haven't been sleeping well for these last few months.'"

"What had her husband to say to that?"

"Simply: 'No? Don't tell me I've been talking again?' "

"Talking in his sleep?"

"Sal told him he was talking more than he had ever done—at any rate for over twenty-five years. Then she asked him if his head was troubling him."

"He suffered from head trouble? Neuralgia or some such thing?"

"I'd never heard that he did, but he was badly scarred about the left temple."

"Did he admit to headaches when his wife was questioning him?"

"He simply said it was nothing like that and that he would move into the spare room for a bit, but Sal refused to let him, even though he insisted that if he were disturbing her or keeping her awake it would be the best plan."

"And that was everything you overheard?"

"There was some more. Technical stuff about what he was doing in the workshop that made the drill scream so much. I can't remember that part of it very well, but Eric will be able to tell you. All I know is that we were in stitches because at one point I'm sure he kissed her and she said: 'Canoodling in public? At our age?' It really did sound funny."

"Did Harte reply?"

"No. Sal went on to say she was rather pleased she was up early after all because it was a lovely day. It all sounded so very nice and cosy and . . ."

"And?"

"I was going to say safe."

Masters grimaced. "I think you were right. It should have been safe. Safe as Happy Families—till

Mister Poison the Assassin popped up. By the way, had the Hartes any family?"

Mrs Summerbee shook her head, and the curls bobbed. "Sal wanted children—could have had them—but Roger couldn't oblige."

"Infertility? Or his disability?"

"He couldn't perform. Whether or not they could have used AI or not, I don't know. But I don't suppose it was on when Sal would have wanted it."

"You say Mrs Harte wanted children?"

"Of her own—and Roger's. She didn't want to adopt."

"That sounds as if she was more strongly attached to him than is the case with many childless couples."

"They were devoted to each other. Not in a mawkish way. She looked after him like a child. He adored her. It was plain for everybody to see, but it never inhibited them or made others feel uncomfortable. Roger going like this has been a real blow to everybody in Lowther, Mr Masters."

"And yet somebody killed him."

"I can only think of one person that could be."

"Mr Rencory?"

"Detestable man! Really detestable."

"But even he liked Mr Harte, I believe."

"He certainly had every reason to. If it hadn't been for Roger . . ."

"What would have happened, Mrs Summerbee?"

"Everybody would have . . . ostracised him and his wife."

"Frozen them out of local society?"

"Yes." She was adamant about it. "We'd have ignored them. Pointedly. Shown him he wasn't wanted."

"Why?"

The question came as a shock to her. Mrs Summerbee looked at him in bewilderment. "Why?" she echoed.

Masters nodded.

"Because he is impossible. He's a thick-necked, red-faced, uncouth lout. If he's a self-made man, all I can say is he didn't do a very good job on himself."

"A brazen image?"

"You could put it that way. Certainly brass—as he calls it—is the only god."

Masters tamped his pipe and drew on it a little harder to revive the remaining embers of tobacco. He was feeling uneasy. Jenny Summerbee was patently a kind-hearted woman. She appeared to have a sense of humour. She was candid, in that she confessed to overhearing her neighbours' conversation. She gave the impression of being a good reporter. She was a personable woman and had undoubtedly been a very pretty girl. People like her—in Masters' experience—fought shy of being bitchy about other people without good reason. They'd been brought up to think it not quite nice to be censorious. But Rencory had assuredly got up her nose. Was his attitude to blame? His appearance? Or his actions? He decided he'd better ask.

"Everything about him is horrid," she replied. "He blusters, you know."

"A lot of men do that, but they are not universally hated."

"That's true. We've got our fair share of pomposity here in Lowther as you can imagine. It's a haven for a cross-section of the community with the top and bottom lopped off. Like you get in diving events, where you have seven judges and the highest and lowest marks are disregarded to prevent extremes being counted. Do you know what I mean?"

Masters smiled. "I would say that's a very apt simile, Mrs Summerbee. At any rate it gives me the picture."

"What I'm trying to say is that the Lowther Blimp, as a species, is a gentleman with it. They have standards, some of which may be regarded as foolish today. The country may be going to the dogs, by gad, but Lowther will never resort to either the greyhound track or to the level of the dirty tykes. And, of course, not all our menfolk are blimps."

"Rencory just doesn't measure up to your standards of courtesy, pleasantness, political affiliation and so on?"

"Something of the sort—but not quite as nebulous as that. He is positively offensive. Swears at people. And then there was the question of the short-cut."

Scenting some local talking point, Masters said he would like to hear about the short-cut.

"Norman and Pam Nicol used to live at twenty-seven before Rencory bought it. Norman was moved to Scotland by his firm—something to do with the discovery of oil near Aberdeen. Quite a shock to us all, really, because Norman was in his late fifties and lived in the Close for more than twenty years."

"Another popular man?"

"Not quite in Roger's class, but then, you see, he didn't have the advantages of a disability."

Masters thought about this one as Jenny Summerbee prattled on. A disability, he thought, was not usually an aid to popularity. Rather the reverse in his experience. But probably Roger Harte had learned to make full use of the drawback.

"Norman was president of the tennis club." She got

to her feet and again moved to the french window. "You can see the fence surrounding the courts from here. And the clubhouse." She pointed directly down her own garden. Running across the backs of all the gardens in this semicircular end of the Close was a high, chicken wire fence. He could just make it out above the thick hedge and between the trees planted to hide it. The clubhouse was no more than a visible smudge of what looked like creosoted planking topped by bright green felt tiles.

"Do you and your husband play?"

"Oh, yes. Practically everybody does. And those that don't are members of the club."

"Nice and handy for you."

"Ah!" She looked round at him. "It used to be."

"I don't understand."

She made her way back to the sofa. "To get to the clubhouse by road from here is a journey of more than two miles. Nothing in a car, perhaps, but two-car families are a very recent thing. Wives who wanted to play when their husbands were away with the car were faced with either a long walk or the fag of cadging a lift. So Norman Nicol applied for permission to put a gate in his back hedge and for right of way across the little stream. He then built a tiny bridge over the ditch and we all used to use his garden as right of way to the club. We just used to slip down the side of the house, down the garden path, over the bridge and we were there—right on court number three."

"Very convenient. What happened when Rencory came?"

"He refused to let us go that way. He sealed up the gate."

Masters had seen this coming. Rencory's action would obviously offend his neighbours. But was the fault all on Rencory's side? Masters would have been willing to bet that the inhabitants of the Close had assumed that they could continue to use the short-cut without reference to Rencory. He would not be in the least surprised if nobody had mentioned it to the new owner whose first inkling of what went on was probably the sight of a bevy of strangers making free of his garden. Any man might be excused for taking high-handed action in the circumstances.

"And has he kept it sealed?"

"Ever since, despite polite approaches."

"From whom?"

"Roger Harte for one. He's secretary of the club. Was, I mean. Rencory's action was a great nuisance to everybody."

Masters stood up. He looked down at her. "If it was such a great nuisance, Mrs Summerbee, why didn't Mr Harte take the obvious step?"

"Obvious step? You mean go to law, or something?"

"Nothing quite so drastic. His ground marches with Rencory's. Why not put a gate in his own hedge and have the short-cut transferred to his own garden?"

She put a hand to her mouth and opened her eyes wide in surprise. "Do you know, I never thought of that."

"Perhaps not. But it must have occurred to Mr Harte. I wonder why he didn't do it?"

And Masters really was wondering why. As he left the house he was trying to decide why Harte, as the one man in the Close with any time for Rencory—and, therefore, presumably with any influence on the man—had not succeeded in persuading his neighbour to keep the short-cut open or, failing that, had not opened up an alternative entrance from his own garden.

Green had gone to call on the neighbour on the other side of Rencory's house. He, like Masters, was not looking forward to the interview. But for different reasons. True, he was sticky and hot. His suit was too heavy for the weather, so the heat bothered him. But not as much as other things. So far, Green had had a bad day. His incipient summer cold, the unnerving experience in the traffic, his quarrel with DI Woodside, had all combined to depress him. But chiefly he hated the ambience of this enquiry. He was as sensitive to middle-class atmosphere as a bug on a Petri dish is to an antibiotic. Green was more at home among what he was pleased to term working classes and which Hill described with more exactitude as the loafing classes. Not that Hill was unkind to genuine work-people, but the type which it was usually Green's lot to investigate were those euphemistically described as 'of no visible means of support'. The invisible means were invariably the fruits of crime and other people's labours. Green knew this and was well aware of what made such people tick. Consequently he was at his happiest when dealing with them. Allied to a left-wing political belief which seemed to permeate his every thought and action, this proclivity left him uneasy in an atmosphere such as he could sense in Lowther Close.

Hermione Stockwell answered his ring. From the moment he saw her, Green knew he wasn't going to like her. She was too tall and slim. Green's preference was for the plumper type. He liked to see well-filled thighs and protruberant bosoms. He considered it a waste of female flesh if it was fashioned in any other way. Had he been a potter, all Green's clay would have been moulded into swag-bellied urns, with never a sign of a slender specimen vase.

Her voice was deep, as though she leaned on each breath. Green considered the measured tones to be mere affectation and guessed they were the end product of an expensive finishing school education rather than Mrs Stockwell's own natural merchandise. He was irritated by them.

"Scotland Yard, ma'am. Detective Inspector Green."

She seemed unimpressed. "Do you wish to speak to me?"

"I wouldn't be here else, would I?" He was deliberately making his own thick voice gruffer as if the laws of nature were working overtime to preserve the tonal balance in this encounter.

"I shall be happy to help in any way I can—if you will identify yourself first."

"Very wise," grunted Green, fishing with a sticky hand in the depths of his inside breast pocket.

When she was satisfied he was the genuine article she led him inside. The sitting room was flooded with sunlight. The chintz covers—cream background with the blue delphiniums dominating the red of roses and the green of foliage—looked as cool and inviting as anything in the way of furnishing that Green could remember.

Hermione Stockwell had obviously been hand-sewing. Her needles and cotton were on the coffee table, while a small pile of socks and other neatly folded garments was on the sofa. She sat down beside them and picked up a shirt.

"Please sit down. You won't mind if I sew on a button while we talk."

It was a statement, not a question. Green had no reply. He sank heavily into an armchair that seemed to be stuffed with down. He was cosseted by it. The comfort, paradoxically, made him feel more ill at ease. He leaned forward to pull up his socks, being conscious that they were wrinkled round his ankles and that his position in the chair was such that he must be showing a length of hairy bare leg. Green was prudish about such things.

"If you are hot," said Mrs Stockwell, "I shan't mind if you take your jacket off, so long as you are not wearing braces."

Green was wearing braces. He stayed as he was.

"May I know your name, ma'am?"

"Hermione Stockwell. My husband is Patrick Stockwell. He is with a Merchant Bank in the City."

Green's private thought at so full an answer was that this one knew her onions. She was a cool one. Literally. In simple royal blue skirt, white shirt blouse open at the neck, short sleeves, bare legs and blue and white sandals, she could have just emerged from a cold shower. Her hair was dark and page-boy length, centre parted. Her skin a gypsy brown. Features slightly pointed, with no excess flesh.

"Thank you, Mrs Stockwell. I suppose you know why I'm here?"

"You're in Lowther, I presume, to investigate Roger Harte's death. Your reason for being in my house escapes me."

"I'd best explain. Our information so far is that Mr Harte was above average popular as a man."

"Quite right." She centred the button on its thread

and held it in place with her thumb. "He was a gentleman not only in every sense of the word, but in the best sense."

"I don't get that. Every sense should cover the best in my book."

"Maybe. But there are degrees of perfection. Roger Harte was in a league by himself."

"Above your own husband?"

"Yes." She made no bones about her reply. But she guessed his surprise. "That doesn't meant that I would ever have exchanged my husband for Roger Harte. Perfection is not always lovable, Mr Green. I love my husband—with all his few faults."

Green warmed slightly towards her. "You're saying your husband is human, where Mr Harte was not?"

"Not at all." She picked up the scissors to cut the thread. "Roger Harte was very human. Very human. But I would have found him uncomfortable as a husband."

"You're losing me again. Do you mean because of his physical disabilities?"

"Nothing like that." She laid the shirt on the cushion beside her to fold it neatly. "I am a woman of very definite likes and dislikes. I like to indulge them. My husband panders to my feelings. Aids and abets them, in fact, as he is very like me and, strangely enough, his tastes for the most part match mine." She patted the folded shirt and then looked directly at Green. He could see her eyes were dark blue. "Roger Harte was so good that he would never have indulged, let alone participated in, my loves and hates. He would have tried to iron them out to a bland acceptance which would have meant that I would never have plumbed the depths of a jolly good hate, but then neither would I ever have scaled the heights of enthusiasm. Does that make sense to you?"

"I get the drift. But Harte himself was one of your likes, was he?"

"Most certainly. I could appreciate all his goodness and kindness so long as it did not affect my private feelings."

"I've heard that this chap Rencory who owns the house between you and Harte is disliked pretty much by his neighbours, yet Harte died in his house."

"A perfect illustration of my point, Inspector. I hate Rencory, as everybody else does, except that Roger didn't. Or wouldn't. He tried to be friendly with Rencory, and tried to get others to accept him."

"How successful was Mr Harte?"

"To date? Not very. But he would have been. Roger's charm would have won the day sooner or later, at any rate with some people."

"But not with you?"

"I don't think so. As I told you, I recognised this power in Roger and it rather tended to make me more determined to resist."

"And your husband?"

"Patrick? He's as stubborn as I am."

"So he dislikes Rencory, too."

"Can't stand the man. But he thought the world of Roger Harte."

Green had cooled off a bit. He could still feel his shirt sticking to his back, but his forehead was no longer running with sweat. He felt in his pocket for the crumpled pack of Kensitas, then thought better of it as he wasn't sure there'd be two cigarettes left, and even if there were, he didn't feel he could offer this dame a bent fag.

He was a little disconcerted to find she had guessed his intention. She rose to her feet and fetched an alabaster cigarette box from the mantlepiece. It was full—probably fifty or sixty in it. All as neat and tidy as the rest of the house appeared to be. She stood over him, offering the open box.

"Ta!" He was very conscious of her nearness. She was so clean, so cool, so delicately perfumed that his senses were offended. He felt so self-conscious that he was clumsy with the matchbox and felt foolish holding the light up high as she bent over slightly to reach the flame.

She placed an ashtray on a stand beside his chair and returned to her seat.

"What exactly are you hoping to discover by talking to me, Mr Green?"

"I dunno yet, ma'am."

"Truthful if not completely reassuring."

"You could probably help by telling me why you hate Mr Rencory."

"Can you spare the rest of the day?"

"Just as long as you like. But not if all you're going to tell me is that he picked his nose in public and called a napkin a serviette."

She laughed. It was the first sign of humour there'd been. "I think you have hidden depths, Mr Green. Or do I mean that you see more than you would have one believe?"

"P'raps it's because we get to know people in our job, ma'am. I mean the real people under the veneer."

"Have I revealed my real self at all?"

"Not so's you'd notice, ma'am, but I'd say you were of Irish extraction . . ."

She opened her eyes at that one. "Now how on earth can you tell that?"

"Well," said Green, "your husband's name is Patrick which is a bit Paddy." He was feeling more pleased with himself.

"Yes."

"And you've got black hair and blue eyes which often come with an Irish strain."

"Interesting. But my voice is not Irish."

"No-o. But you could have got rid of the brogue at some posh school. Yes, that's it. At a convent. You're Irish and Roman Catholic."

She didn't give him the satisfaction of telling him he was right, but merely said, as she stubbed out her cigarette: "That just shows one should never underestimate a gentleman from the Yard." She looked up. "Is our conversation at an end?"

"Not quite. You still haven't given your reasons for hating Mr Rencory."

"You're insisting on that, are you?"

"Only on solid facts—if there are any."

"All right. You shall have just one instance. An episode that cost my husband over a hundred pounds. That will help to explain why Patrick hates Rencory, too." She got to her feet. "Would you care to come with me for a moment?"

She led him through the french window on to a little paved terrace.

"These houses in the circular part of the Close are built in segments of a circle. All our gardens are wedge shaped, with the points cut off."

Green nodded. "If they weren't cut off, they'd all meet in the centre of that little plot in the middle of the road."

"That's right. Now look at our boundary fence on Rencory's side."

Green followed the line of her finger. The ranch type fence of horizontal, widely-shaped boards was painted white, and seemed to run away to the right as it diverged from the one which separated the Stockwell's garden from the attached house on its left. Green got the picture even more clearly now. Each pair of houses—as opposed to each single one—was in a segment of land. The dividing fence ran straight out from the buildings at right angles. Only the outer ones opened out so that the gardens were wider at the bottom than the top.

"When the wind is in the north-west," said Hermione Stockwell, "it blows direct over Rencory's back hedge, but on to our house."

Green could appreciate that the offset effect of the layout could mean just that.

"Now," she went on, "look to the bottom left hand corner of the Rencory garden and what do you see?"

"Nothing much. Only a heap of garden rubbish."

"Exactly. But when the Rencorys moved in, that grew to be half the size of a haystack, with all sorts of packing material—boxes and cardboard."

"Go on." He said glumly. He could guess what had happened.

"It stayed like that for months—an eyesore."

He knew she would object to that. Her own garden was as neat as the house. Well trimmed lawn, well tended beds with a high summer show of colour.

She turned towards the house. "You see all our paintwork is white."

Green nodded. It was brilliant white, glistening in the sun.

"The final coat was put on late one Friday afternoon in the spring. The next morning the wind was in the north-west."

"Don't tell me," said Green. "Rencory lit his bonfire."

"And treated it with something that sent heavy smoke and smuts right on to our new paintwork which was not yet hard."

"Treated it? What with?"

"I'd have said with old, heavy sump oil. There was certainly dense smoke and clouds of unburnt carbon particles coming from it in great gouts, but there wasn't the sulphurous smell you get with burnt oil."

"No? What did it smell like?"

"A bit rubbery. But mostly of chlorine."

"You know about chlorine?"

"Chlorinated water in the swimming baths and powders for drains."

"Always use liquid disinfectant myself."

"What's that got to do with it?"

"With what?"

"The fact that our paintwork was ruined? We had to have the decorators back to rub it down and give it a new final coat. As I said, it cost over a hundred pounds, just for the back of the house."

"It would do. Especially if this fence was included."

"It was. So now do you see why my husband and I are not the best of friends with the Rencorys?"

They returned to the sitting room. Green asked: "What did your husband do about it?"

"He tackled Rencory. But Rencory said he and his wife had been out of the house all day since early morning and he had not started the fire."

"Did you believe him?"

"What could we do? He *was* away that day. So were we for a lot of the time. And the fire wasn't going when we left. But the paintwork was spoiled by the time we got back. We found Roger Harte trying to put the fire out."

"Alone?"

She nodded. "He said he'd been working in the front of his house and hadn't noticed the fire earlier. It hadn't occurred to him to call for help."

This time Green did fish out his Kensitas. There were three in the packet. She refused his offer on the excuse that he was short. He smoked alone, thoughtful for a moment or two.

"You say you accepted Rencory's story?"

"Privately, no. Nobody else could have set light to his bonfire. He had the front gates locked against intruders whenever they both went out, and the back gate which used to lead to the tennis courts was done away with. No child or mischievous person could have got in there."

"Mr Harte did."

She paused for a moment before replying. Green was of the opinion that this was a thought which had not previously occurred to her.

"So he did. I think he must have pushed his way through a gap in the hedge. There's no fence between their two gardens."

"A disabled man?"

"He was quite . . . spry, I think is the term. At any rate he had a hose pipe."

"He was damping it down?"

"No. He hadn't got as far as turning the water on. I went to do that."

"I see. What did Rencory say when you pointed

out that the heap had oil or rubber—probably old tyres—on it?"

"He denied it. Said there was nothing but garden rubbish, paper, straw, wood and cardboard."

"Nothing to make the smoke, the sooty izals and the smell you complained of?"

"According to Rencory."

"Did you complain to the police?"

"Patrick spoke to Inspector Woodside about it. Not officially, of course. The Inspector said there was nothing he could do. The fire was not within thirty feet of the highway and we'd have to prove Rencory set light to it and so on."

"Not much help then? Didn't come and look at it?"

"He said he'd have to ask Rencory's permission to enter his property, which he knew he wouldn't get."

Green got to his feet. "Thank you, Mrs Stockwell. You've helped me get the picture."

"Are you proposing to arrest Mr Rencory?"

"Not unless we get something more definite to connect him with the murder than bonfires and spoiled paintwork. But don't you worry about who's going to be arrested. It's early days yet."

But in spite of his reassuring words, Green had the impression that Hermione Stockwell was worried about this murder. But for the life of him he could not produce a theory as to why she should be unless her husband was implicated in some way. Green decided he might have to call on Patrick Stockwell later.

Chapter IV

Hill and Brant were foraging together. Both had tried houses and got no reply.

"Not to be wondered at," said Hill. "On a day like this, if I wasn't at work, I'd have the kids out in the country or at the seaside."

"Picnics down the river," said Brant. "No distance at all from here."

Hill grunted. They turned together into the gate of number twelve. As they approached the door, it was opened by a man in grey slacks and short-sleeved white shirt with an open neck.

"Scotland Yard?" No preamble or beating about the bush. A disconcerting directness that caught the sergeants unawares. They both said yes together, like plant-pot men.

"Names?"

"Sergeant Hill. This is Sergeant Brant."

"Weeks-Baine. Captain RN, retired." The introductions were over.

"Want to talk to me?"

"If you please, sir."

"Come in." The eyes twinkled. "Don't worry, I'm not going to say welcome aboard or come over the brow. I can speak without using naval jargon."

The sergeants stepped inside the cool hall.

"Sitting room," ordered Weeks-Baine, indicating the way. "The sun's in there. Make yourselves comfortable and I'll bring some limers. 'Spect you could do with some."

He disappeared down the narrower passage beside the staircase, obviously making for the kitchen.

"No jargon," murmured Hill, "and then he goes for limers. I'll bet he offers us a tickler when he gets back."

The captain reappeared, bearing a tray with a large glass jug full of lime juice with ice and three tumblers.

"Can I pour for you?"

"Please, sir."

The ice tinkled, the liquid flowed.

"Now, what d'you want specifically? Know it's to do with poor old Roger Harte's death in general, of course. Cheers!" He raised his glass and then took a chair facing the sergeants.

"It's a little too early for us to be specific, sir," said Hill. "We're just reconnoitring at the moment, you might say."

"Good way to proceed. Who's your CO?"

"Detective Superintendent Masters."

"Good chap, is he?"

"The best there is."

"I'd heard so. Glad to know you confirm it. Roger Harte was an outstanding man, too. Loved the feller.

In the right way, of course. Loved him. So did my wife and married daughter."

"Did you have much to do with him, sir?" Brant was wanting to find out as quickly as possible how valuable this particular confrontation might be.

Weeks-Baine grinned, as if he guessed Brant's thought. "Living in Turbary or the Close is like living on a ship, Sergeant. That's why I like it. Closed community. Know everybody in it. Know what the other feller's likely to do in given circumstances. In other words, know where you are in a world that doesn't know where it is these days. Get me so far?"

Brant nodded.

"Good. Follows then, one can't help having a lot to do with most people in the community. Had a lot to do with Harte. Gregarious character, Harte. In and into everything in the best possible way. Dined here about once a month. Sunday evenings mostly."

"Ah!" said Hill. "That doesn't surprise me."

"No?"

"Sunday evening is the traditional time for officers to entertain on board, isn't it, sir?"

"Quite right. Carried on the habit. Can't stand Sundays if there's not a bit of jollification to look forward to. Always have guests on Sundays evenings. Recognised by others in the Close as our night."

"So Mr Harte was a frequent visitor, and presumably he returned the compliment."

"Like clockwork. Met very often on other evenings, of course. Club, Gleaner, other houses."

"Did you ever entertain Mr Rencory, sir?"

"Once. Did the civil thing. Invited the newcomer. Never again."

"Why not, sir?"

Weeks-Baine pursed his mouth. His eyes darkened. "Dunno, actually. Nothing you could put your finger on. Just generally boorish. Out of his depth, I suppose. Shouldn't have been. Feller's made his way in the world. So not a fool. Failed to learn rudiments of manners. No politeness."

"Any examples, sir?"

"Told us how much his wife's frock had cost before he'd been in the house two minutes. Embarrassed the woman. Mousey type, you know, Mrs R. Dominated by him. Completely dominated. Knew her husband was making *faux pas* left, right and centre. Particularly when he said he'd seen the model my wife was wearing in CA modes and asked how much she'd been rushed for it. His words, not mine."

"As you say, sir, very embarrassing for the ladies."

"Not for my wife. She told him how much she'd paid. Think she said she'd got two in a job lot for a tenner. That got him. Knew he was being ribbed. Bumptious bloke. Like the poet johnny says, I don't care for all one sees that's Japanese. Saw too much of them in the last struggle. Rencory dotes on 'em. Thinks they're destined to be world leaders. That sort of thing. Highly offensive to old Horace Fraser who was here and had been in Jap hands most of the war."

"Perhaps Mr Rencory didn't know that," said Brant.

"Course he did. That's how the subject came up—Horace's incarceration. Rencory just laughed at him. Laughed at sufferin' that nearly cost the man his life. I ask you?"

"He sounds insufferable, sir."

"Right word for him, Sergeant. Insufferable."

"So you've never had him round here since?" asked Hill.

"Had him round—uninvited. Two or three weeks ago. Sunday evening. Last time Roger and Sally Harte dined with us, in fact."

"You say he came uninvited, sir?"

"Came knocking on the door with some story about his blasted television set not working."

"Could we have the full story, sir, please?"

Weeks-Baine got to his feet, refilled the glasses and offered them cigarettes. When they were all smoking he sat down to tell them of the incident.

"Damned cheek," he announced. "Fellow Rencory had the biggest goggle-box in the district. Would have. He's that type. Then another, bigger one comes on the market. Colour—and Japanese—of course. The very latest in vulgarity. Remote controls or some such malarky. Rencory decides to install. Lets everybody know it's coming, of course. Saturday morning, pantechnicon arrives with this affair. Rencory running around to pipe it over the side and wave farewell to the old one. Great to-do. Expected us to line the rails, I shouldn't wonder. Didn't, of course."

He paused to stub out his cigarette.

"Anyhow, safely installed. Rencory uses it on Saturday. Hauls various people in to watch. Marvellous. Tells everybody he never watches on Sundays until religious clap-trap is over at about half past seven. Then his favourite programme comes on. Some sort of serial. Says he wouldn't miss it for a hundred pounds—that sort of thing.

"Roger and Sally dining with us that evening. Just sat down to table. Last quarter of the second dog. Right time to feed. Relaxed. Knock at door. Answer it. Rencory in a lather demanding to know if my wife was using unsuppressed hairdryer or some such gadget. Told him to ask elsewhere. Got the impression he had been going round everybody in the Close, accusin' 'em. Damn silly! Sunday evening, trying to find somebody using an egg whisk."

Hill broke in: "What was his trouble, sir? Did he say?"

"Damn goggle-box was playing him up. Snowstorm or something on the screen. Couldn't view his blasted programme. Convinced it was somebody close by using some electrical apparatus that was causing it."

"What happened, sir?"

"Roger Harte came to the door. Napkin in hand. Offered to go and look at set. In the middle of dinner! I ask you?"

"Was Mr Harte something of an expert on TV, sir?"

"Clever as a boffin. Was a boffin, in fact. He tottered off with Rencory."

"Did you ever learn the result?"

"When Harte got back. He'd gone in, taken the back off the set and asked Rencory for a screwdriver or pliers or something. Rencory only had what Roger called Cobbler's tools. Harte used to using precision instruments, you know. Decided he'd have to go into his own quarters next door for what he wanted. Warned Rencory not to touch the set with the back off and not to switch on. Got back a couple of minutes later with a roll of tools. Tinkered about inside for a minute or so. Switched on. Perfect picture. Screwed the back on—said he couldn't trust Rencory to do it. Came back here to finish dinner."

"Mr Harte must have been an amiable man, sir."

"The best. I'd have seen Rencory in hades before I'd have interrupted a social evening to mend his box. Done it the next morning, perhaps, but not there and then. Roger probably couldn't wait to get his hands on it. Still, he would put himself out for anybody. Too damn soft-hearted in some ways."

"Why should anybody wish to murder such a man, sir?"

"Beats me. World we live in, I suppose. Everything arseytarsey these days. Cosset the criminal who murders the good man."

"So you've not had anything to do with Mr Rencory since this TV incident three weeks ago, sir?" asked Brant.

"Seen the feller drive to and fro in his car. German make, of course. Big Mercedes. Chap like Rencory wouldn't buy British. Nothing more than that."

"And Mr Harte?"

"Met him a score of times since. I go in and do a bit to his garden now and then. Like gardens an' I'm here all day." Weeks-Baine sounded as though he was apologising for doing a good turn. "Roger not fit enough to use spade and hoe. So help him out a bit. Tidy him up once or twice a week. Work alongside Sally an' do the heavy stuff, if you get me."

"Perfectly, sir, thank you. So there's no light you can throw on the actual murder?"

"None. Rencory would be my first choice, of course, but can't honestly say that even he would do down a feller like Roger Harte. Mustn't prejudge even him. As I say, wouldn't know what to suggest, but'd like a chance to boot whoever did it fair an' square in the slats." The old sailor's face reddened with momentary emotion.

"Quite, sir." Hill got to his feet. "Thank you very much for talking to us and for your hospitality."

"Pleasure. Don't get much chance for a gas during the day. Like to buy you a drink if I see you in The Gleaner."

"We're booked in there, sir."

"Champion! Not bad grub. A bit pricey, perhaps, but wholesome. Make a good Pickwick pie. Try it if it's on the menu while you're there."

"Thanks for the tip, sir."

"Steak and oysters in it. Oysters cheaper than the beef these days." Weeks-Baine ushered them out of the room, into the hall and towards the open front door. "Good day to you. An' good hunting."

Masters was standing close to the ornamental patch in the middle of the Close. He was appreciating a mixed bed of white geraniums and red petunias, smoking a new pipe of Warlock Flake, thinking over his conversation with Mrs Summerbee, wondering where to go next and waiting for Green. The earlier reluctance to get along with the case was disappearing. He put that down to the fact that the sun, though still high, was nevertheless westering, and there were now some shadows thrown by the houses. They hadn't so far actually cooled the atmosphere, but they gave the impression of doing so.

He was also turning over in his mind the paradox that Harte had not opened up a way through his own garden to the tennis club. He was toying with an idea. Perhaps Harte had deliberately refrained from stepping in for a good reason. If he—Harte—had been a good psychologist as well as a good man, it could have meant that by holding off himself, he could even-

tually persuade Rencory to climb down and, in doing
so, establish some sort of relationship with the neighbours. Harte had probably thought that as soon as an
alternative route had been opened up, the opportunity for Rencory to reinstate himself would be gone
for ever. That's how it could have been. But Masters
doubted it. From all he had learned so far, he judged
Harte to have been pragmatic in community affairs—
as opposed to business ones. The mere fact that he
was so well liked by everybody suggested that he was
at least interested—if not prepared to meddle in—
other people's affairs. So it meant Harte was a practical man, actively engaged in finding solutions to life's
little problems—as witness his efforts on behalf of disabled people. So he should—if Masters had judged him
aright—have opened up a new way to the tennis club
within hours of hearing that Rencory had closed the
former one. That would have been in character.

Green came out of number twenty-five and stumped
across towards him.

"If what you heard," he said to Masters, "was anything like the stuff I got, you might as well take Rencory in, because this lot round here are determined to
nobble him."

"There was no god but Harte?"

"And no devil but Rencory."

"Are you persuaded?"

"Not by a long chalk. There's a lot of class divi-
siveness about this. Rencory called a spade a bloody
shovel and they prefer it to be referred to as an agri-
cultural instrument."

"Rencory had the opportunity."

"Maybe he did. But we've got no means and motive
yet. And if Rencory's as clever a business man as he

appears to be, he wouldn't have fouled his own nest. He'd have done Harte in a long way from number twenty-seven."

"Unless he was clever enough to realise you'd take that view."

Green took out his packet of Fisherman's Friends, selected one and put it in his mouth. He plainly thought Masters' last remark to be unworthy of comment.

"We'll go inside and compare notes. Then we'll tackle Rencory."

"Together?"

"I'd prefer the two of us there. If we can hear what the sergeants have got as well before we go, so much the better."

Green's greatest asset as a detective was his phenomenal memory. He could—and did—give Masters an almost verbatim account of his interview with Hermione Stockwell. Though Green himself had regarded it merely as a means of gathering background material to help them get the feel of the Close, Masters was quite thoughtful at the end of the recital.

The sergeants had joined them meanwhile. When Green had finished talking about the ruination of the Stockwell paint, Hill gave an account of the interview with Weeks-Baine.

If anything, Masters was even more thoughtful at the end of the account of how Harte had left the dinner table to repair Rencory's television set. He was so quiet that none of the other three spoke for some time. Then it was Green who asked if they were to see Rencory that day or the next.

To Green's surprise—and that of the sergeants—

Masters murmured: "Whom God would destroy He first sends mad."

Green looked across at the sergeants and raised his eyebrows. But Hill and Brant were not prepared to agree with the implied assertion that Masters had left his trolley. So often in the past this man had amazed them by his thought processes, many of which had seemed to stem from something as equally irrelevant as this murmured quotation.

"Come again?"

"Sorry. Mind wandering. We'll go next door now. Hill, you and Brant scout around and try to get some information about Harte's mechanical activities. I'm interested in what he actually did. Did he mend all the TV sets in Lowther? Or just Rencory's? Did he mend the kids' toys—engines and the like that went wrong? What part did he actually play in the lives of these people in Lowther?"

They all four left number twenty-eight together. There seemed to be slightly more activity now, after the sleep of the afternoon. Down the road a number of small children were tumbling from a car. The driver, a mother who had collected her own brood and several others from school, called to them as they scampered off, and then stood and watched to see that each reached its own home safely. A milkman was busy. His float, half empty, purring slowly into the circle of the Close.

"Home time," said Green. "The best time at school. Lord, how I used to like it. Scarpering home for tea. If it wasn't ready I used to get a slice of bread and dripping. Pork dripping was best, with the brown bottoms and a scatter of salt. I don't suppose any one of those kids ever tasted anything half so good as a slice of bread and drip. They'll get a glass of milk and a chocolate wafer to last them through, I suppose."

Hill said: "You're right. I'd prefer a lump of crusty loaf to a chocolate biscuit any day."

Green looked pleased. "At least you know what's good for you, lad."

"If we've finished the gastronomic reminiscences . . ."

Green took the hint, opened the gate of number twenty-seven and, with his usual bad manners, preceded Masters up the path to the front door.

Rencory's appearance came as no surprise.

They'd been led to expect a bull-necked, red-faced, square-built character. And that's what they got. Fair hair, turned mousey, and cut short up the sides, plastered down on top. An unsuitable floral shirt open to the navel and displaying a mat of hair on chest and belly. Trendy tight trousers in pale blue with a hint of silver in the weave showed off the ample buttocks. Pale yellow socks peeped coyly through the interstices of champagne-coloured, basket-weave pumps.

"Are you the police?"

Masters introduced Green and himself, said he had come to speak to Rencory and would rather do it inside the house than out.

"Come in, then. You're lucky to find me at home. I'm usually at business at this time."

"But not on the day after a chap's been murdered in your house?" asked Green, stepping inside.

"Who said it was murder?" asked Rencory, shutting the door behind them. "And if it was who said I had anything to do with it?"

Green suddenly felt happy. This was the sort he

could deal with. "Me. In answer to both questions. Now, how about somewhere to confab?"

Masters waited for it, and it came. "We'll talk in the lounge." He'd have laid odds against Rencory saying sitting room.

This room, oddly enough, was not quite as plastic and plush as he would have expected. He'd have guessed at modern heavy glass, so-called executive toys, cocktail cabinet and meaningless daubs. Mrs Rencory had avoided the lot. True, the room shrieked of expensive furnishing, but it was not outrageous. It was nothing. There'd been no plan and little taste in the choosing of the pieces, so that they did not blend harmoniously. But taken separately, each piece was pleasing enough. Masters was reminded of a remark which he dimly associated with Oscar Wilde to the effect that if there was one thing worse than bad taste, it was no taste at all. He felt he couldn't agree; but then, he could never be a Wilde devotee. And at least Mrs Rencory had provided large, man-sized armchairs and this, for a man of Masters' proportions, went a long way towards wiping out other unpleasing aspects.

"Apart from what DI Green has just said, nobody has yet suggested that you are implicated in the death of Mr Harte beyond the fact that he died here in your house," said Masters as he sat down.

"Oh, yes they have."

"Not the police, surely?"

"No, but the rest of Lowther has."

"They've accused you?"

"Not to my face. They daren't. But I know what goes on." Rencory flipped open a cigarette box, picked one out and lit it savagely with a table lighter:

a chunky plastic model with bogus pieces-of-eight embedded in it. He did not offer the box to either of them. Green pointedly took out his crumpled Kensitas packet, looked in and found it empty, and put it on the coffee table. Still Rencory didn't take the hint.

"How do you know?" asked Masters mildly.

"They've made it plain enough. They don't want to know Maisie and me, and I could buy and sell the lot of them."

"If nobody wanted to know you, why was Mr Harte in your house last night?"

"Old Rodge was different. He was ready to be pally. We liked him."

"The most popular man in Lowther, we understand."

"Yeah! Rodge was popular, OK. Like I said, he was a decent bloke."

"He, at least, showed you friendship."

"That's right. He was the only one, so why should I kill him?"

Masters took out his pipe. "Mr Rencory, you must not assume that we necessarily regard you as a murderer. It puts you at a disavantage and hampers our enquiries."

"How?"

"It inhibits profitable discussion and colours all you have to say. Now ease off a bit and try to talk calmly."

Rencory stubbed out the half-finished cigarette and turned to Masters. "All right. So I can trust you. You're wanting to get at the truth . . ."

"Without fear or favour."

". . . but you're here, grilling me."

"Hardly that, sir. I've not even asked you what

happened last night, let alone anything about yourself."

"You're like the people round here. Never say what you mean, and talk behind your back."

Masters pressed home the Warlock Flake before replying. "You know, Mr Rencory, you wouldn't like it one little bit if I did say what I think."

"No? Try me."

"You're ill-mannered—shown by the fact that you helped yourself to a cigarette without offering them round."

"What? What's that?"

"You're purse-proud—shown by the fact that you told us within two minutes of meeting you that you can buy and sell half of Lowther."

"Here . . . you . . . !"

"Shall I go on saying what I think and mean, Mr Rencory, or will that suffice to show you that sometimes it is wise and kind to temper one's conversation?"

Rencory snorted. "You're a clever bastard."

"Clever perhaps."

"Look," said Green. "You've got a boulder on your shoulder because folk round here are toffee-nosed. I'll give you a tip. When in Rome! Now take me. If I go into a posh hotel I'm not used to, I don't go calling the odds round the foyer. I look, listen and learn. And that's what you don't do—learn. So why not start now, matey, with us? Just talk natural, don't assume we're here to do you down even if you're not guilty of murder . . ."

"Which I'm not."

"Fine. So why come out fighting? You're only giving folk the wrong impression—us as well your lah-di-dah neighbours. And right now's not the time to give anybody the chance of grabbing hold of the wrong end of the stick."

Having finished what he had to say, Green got to his feet and helped himself to one of Rencory's cigarettes. Masters took up the running.

"Why did Mr Harte visit you last evening?"

"For no particular reason. He just dropped in because his missus was away. He often did if she wasn't there."

"Why when she wasn't there?"

"Because Sarah Harte wasn't as friendly as old Rodge. He knew it and we knew it"

"Was she actively hostile to you both?"

"No, but she was a damn sight more friendly to Maisie than she was to me."

"Your wife?"

"That's right."

"So Mrs Harte did visit you from time to time?"

"Not after I got home. She used to come and see Maisie in the daytime—have a cup of coffee together in the kitchen."

"Nothing more than that?"

"No. Like I said, she had quite a bit to do with Maisie. Helped her choose things—curtains and so on."

"Thank you. Now what did Mr Harte usually talk about when he came?"

"Anything and everything. Sometimes about his own business or his time in the army."

"Oh, yes. He was crippled during the war, wasn't he? Did he ever tell you how it happened?"

"Funny thing! He never did."

"Didn't you think that strange? To discuss army life but never mention what must have been the most devastating experience that ever happened to him? One that has affected his whole life ever since?"

Surprisingly, Rencory said: "I guessed he was sensitive about it so I never asked."

"No hint at all?"

Rencory chewed his lower lip for a moment and then said that he had a vague impression that Harte had received his injuries in a tank accident. "He asked me a lot of questions about tanks one night. Where I'd used them and so on."

"You were in the tank corps?"

"I was a Gunner. We used tanks for OP's."

"Was Harte a tank man?"

"No. PBI. He was a Dorset, I think."

Green said: "I was a Gunner, too."

Masters looked across at him. There was something in Green's tone that grated more than usual. Was Green doubtful about Rencory's claims? Or about Harte's?

"So you were an officer?" asked Green sourly.

"What if I was? I was better at the job than a lot I could mention."

"Tell me," said Green. "Were you in the Normandy bridgehead?"

" 'Course I was. Self-propelled, we were."

"Was Mr Harte in the bridgehead?"

"That's where he got the chop."

Masters was even more bewildered. It was fairly clear to him that Green had a reason for these questions, but he, Masters, could not for the life of him see where they were leading.

"What division were you in?"

"Out there? None. We were AGRA."

"Army Group Royal Artillery," explained Green

for Masters' benefit before turning back to Rencory. "So when you weren't thickening up on other people's stonks and barrages, you used to work with independent infantry brigades who had no artillery of their own?"

"That's right, we did. Often."

"We worked with one of them once. The South West Midlands Brigade. Our tanks had gone out of the line for a rest and refit before the Falaise push. They never took us out, though."

"Funny," said Rencory. "We were with that lot just about then. Near that mount or mountain place. Pince something or another."

"Pinçon," supplied Green. "Jerry made a bit of a stand there."

"That's right." Rencory was loosening up visibly. "The day I'm thinking of he was using a hell of a lot of mortars on those poor bloody infantry. I went up to bring some shell fire down on the Jerry positions."

Green turned to Masters. "Sorry. We got rambling on a bit."

"Not to worry. It's a habit with old soldiers. Mr Rencory, to get back to more recent events, are you aware of how Mr Harte died?"

"Poisoning of some sort. It was obvious."

"The doctor didn't say what the poison was?"

"As far as I could make out, he didn't know himself."

"That's true enough. He wasn't absolutely sure. The pathologist positively identified the poison this morning."

"Oh, yes? And what was it?" It was asked as a matter of form, with no real interest.

Masters had no trouble in avoiding a reply. "You

are, I believe, Mr Rencory, a manufacturer of animal foods."

"Cattle feed. Nothing for birds and goldfish. No tinned tasty morsels for lap dogs."

"You've a new factory close by, I understand."

"A few miles away. On the Wistors Road. Modern. All the latest plant."

"You must be very proud of it."

"Of course. It's all come about through my own hard work."

"So you like showing it off to people, do you?"

"Not all that much. People turn their noses up at some of the smells."

"But you have offered to show people round. People from Lowther, I mean."

"Aye, I've offered. Nobody wanted to but Roger Harte and Sarah. They came one afternoon. Spent a couple of hours with us and had a cup of tea in my office."

"Were they interested in what they saw?"

"Now you come to mention it, they were."

"More than you'd have expected them to be?"

"Well, I knew Rodge would want to inspect the plant. Right up his alley. Anything mechanical or electrical always was."

"But Mrs Harte showed interest, too?"

"I hadn't expected her to want to come. I'd said I'd come back here at lunchtime and drive Rodge over. He never drove himself, you know. But Sarah said she'd bring him. Which she did. And she nosed round. Took quite a shine to my senior chemist, Bill Boardman, who showed her round a bit. He's a young-ish bloke with fair hair and blue eyes. The sort the ladies fall for. I was pleased she did. It meant I could spend my time with Rodge on the machinery without her getting bored and impatient. Here, would you like a cuppa tea?"

Green answered: "I'm dying for one. I thought you'd never ask."

"I'll just give Maisie a shout. She's sitting out in the sun. At least she's out in the garden, under the shade of one of those swing seats."

"Please don't disturb her."

"She'll be wanting one herself." Rencory lumbered out of the room. Masters got up to stretch his legs. He didn't look at Green as he said: "You've got ideas about him, haven't you? All that eyewash—swapping wartime reminiscences."

Green grunted and helped himself to another cigarette. "I don't know what I've got, but something's bugging me. So I carried on."

"No luck?"

"Not yet. But I'll remember. Or find somebody who does."

Masters turned to him. "I didn't get all the ins and outs of it, but I jumped to a conclusion."

"Did you now?" It was a sneer. "Without even knowing what I was talking about?"

"It happened to fit in with what I was thinking," said Masters quietly.

"Making the facts fit the theories now, are we? That's rich, coming from you who spend half of your time preaching just the opposite."

"I'll admit it was a leap in the dark. But making facts fit—no! There are no facts. You've just said yourself you can't remember them yet."

Green stretched his legs and yawned without putting his hand over his mouth. Rencory returned.

"Char up in about five. Maisie'll bring it in."

Masters took his chair again. "Thank you. Oh, Mr Rencory, I didn't tell you what the poison was."

"Not to worry. I wouldn't know one from the other."

"So if I tell you it was ricin, it would mean nothing to you?"

"Never heard of it. Strychnine, arsenic and all the crop pesticides, yes. But ricin, never."

"It is very uncommon, I believe. You never told me why Mr Harte visited you last night."

"I did. I told you he was in the habit of dropping in when he was alone."

"I remember that. But had he nothing specific to say? I mean, he came at what could have been your mealtime."

"He knew we didn't have dinner all that much unless we went out for it. Maisie and me, well, we like high tea, rather than spend all night cooking and stacking dishes into the washing up machine."

"No help in the house?"

"Who has? No, Maisie manages. We have a tin of crab or summats like that ready to sit down to when I get home. It suits us."

"So Mr Harte knew enough about your habits not to embarrass you by turning up in the middle of a meal."

"He'd done the same. Had a cold meal and then come across. He said he'd come in the hope of getting a cup of Maisie's coffee instead of going to the trouble of making his own."

"And that's what he had? A cup of coffee?"

"Aye! A proper cup. Not one of those diddy little

things. And there was nothing wrong with the coffee. We all had it. Straight out of the percolator."

"I'm sure it was as good as you say it was." Masters got to his feet as the door opened, and went to help the faded little woman who was manoeuvring a trolley into the room. She seemed to shrink as he approached her with: "Can I help you, ma'am?"

"Oh, it's all right, really."

She had a wowy little voice. The sort of voice which conjured up for him visions of years being the underdog to a domineering husband. And probably enjoying being so.

Masters steered the trolley into the middle of the room.

"Do you want me to pour for you, Milton?"

Masters thought she sounded anxious to please: like a puppy bewildered by the actions of its master and waiting, tail wagging, for some recognisable gesture or phrase to establish reality in the relationship once more.

"Please, love."

There was no lack of affection in the brief reply. It pleased Masters. The woman was all fingers and thumbs as she served them. He handed round for her, talking as he did so. "We're policemen, Mrs Rencory. Detective Inspector Green, and my name's Masters. No, thank you, I won't have a cake, but Mr Green will. He's very fond of the home-made sort, and if you don't watch him he'll clear the plate in no time."

"He's very welcome to." The praise for her baking had eased the tension a little. Green helped. "Just like my old mother used to make. A bit of candied peel in a bun can't be beat, I say. Gives a taste to 'em." He finished the first bun. "Now that's what I call a cake. No brother-where-art-thou? touch about it."

"What's that?" asked Rencory.

"Currants so few and far between they get lonely."

"Maisie's never mingy with the fruit, are you love?"

She smiled. A threadbare wisp of a smile just moved her lips and flickered momentarily in her eyes.

"Sugar, Mr Masters?"

"No thank you."

"Sweetener then? Milton always uses sweeteners." She was getting bolder. She passed her husband the tube of little tablets. "He's supposed to be getting some weight off, but he doesn't seem to manage it."

"He's got a sweet tooth?"

"Ever so. I never take sweet drinks myself."

"I do," said Green, helping himself to four or five lumps.

"Most men seem to," said Maisie Rencory. "Mr Harte did. Sarah was always on to him about it because he didn't get a lot of real exercise, him being a cripple and not able to do a lot."

"Had a pot on him," said Rencory. "Not a very big chap, really, but a definite pot on him. He was another who'd take sweeteners if there wasn't any sugar handy."

"Last night?"

"Yes, last night." Rencory's voice hardened. "But I had 'em, too. And this is the same tube, and I've had several lots today."

"Oh, no," said Maisie. "It couldn't have been anything he got here. I'm ever so careful. Nothing dirty or that's gone off . . ."

"Please don't worry about it, Mrs Rencory." Masters was at his most soothing. "I'm perfectly satisfied that no food and drink you prepared had anything to do with Mr Harte's death."

"He's right there," said Green, wiping crumbs from his lips with the back of his hand. "Otherwise we wouldn't be here having tea with you, would we now? I mean, it stands to reason."

"That makes sense." Rencory sounded mollified. His wife smiled fully. Masters thought she had so little presence that she could probably be with you in a room without you realising you were not alone. Her dress was of unsuitably shiny material, unexceptional in cut and drabness, and tending to make her all one colour from top to toe.

"I'll have another cup just to prove it," said Masters.

A few minutes later Maisie took herself and the trolley off to the kitchen.

"Well," asked Rencory, tossing Green a cigarette. "Is that it then?"

"Just about," said Masters. "But to return to the poison. Ricin. Are you not an industrial chemist yourself?"

"Chemist? Me? Not on your nelly. I'm a sort of cattle food technologist."

"Sort of?"

"I came up the hard way. Self-taught. I learned it all as a foreman in a cake firm before there was all these degrees and things. I saw the way to go ahead about the time there was all that malarky about chlorophyl. You remember? Just after the war? You got it in everything from toothpaste to pills for taking the smell off your breath. That chlorophyl had to be extracted out of good, high quality grass. Mostly Irish.

While it was still green. The pomace that was left was chucked away."

"Pomace?" asked Green.

"The solid refuse: the pulp. I reckoned it could be valuable for winter feed. After all, was just like hay. So I started out buying it for myself. I got it dirt cheap and then I caked it with molasses. It went like . . . well, like hot cakes. That's how I started and I've never looked back."

"Don't they use molasses in silage?" asked Masters.

"That's right. That's where I got my idea from."

"I see. So all your technical research and development are done by qualified industrial chemists."

"Right again. I do admin and sales myself, and keep an eye on the market place so's I can tell the backroom boys what's wanted."

"Then perhaps it will come as a surprise to you to learn that ricin comes from castor oil seeds."

Rencory sat upright in his chair.

"From what?"

"Castor oil seeds."

The man stared at Masters for a moment and then clapped a stubby-fingered hand over his mouth. "Oh, my God," he grated.

Chapter V

It took forty minutes for Boardman to get to Rencory's house. Forty nail-biting minutes for Rencory. Forty minutes during which Maisie Rencory, who had rejoined them, sat in the corner of the sofa and shrank into herself. Pale-faced and frightened-eyed she stared alternately at Masters and Green as though they might rise and strike her.

Masters was playing it cool.

Beyond saying to Rencory: "So you have castor oil seeds at the factory?" and receiving an affirmative nod, he had kept off the subject. Green had wandered over to him and whispered that as it now appeared Rencory had had both the opportunity and the means to commit the murder, shouldn't he now be asked to accompany them to the local station.

Masters had shaken his head. Green's reply had been to remind him that the third of the trio—motive—was the one ingredient in the mix that was optional. It made no difference to Masters' attitude. He refused to ask Rencory to leave his own home even for the temporary office next door. "I'm not risking people seeing him leave for anywhere in our company. I'll not subject him to the gossip until I know he deserves it."

Green sat down and started to chain smoke the cigarettes from Rencory's box. Rencory himself had paled considerably and he was now sweating but silent. Masters deliberately brought him out of deep thought by starting an irrelevant conversation.

"Have you any hobbies?"

"Hobbies?" Rencory was having difficulty in orientating his mind. "No. Never had time for them."

"No golf, tennis, boating, fishing? You're ideally placed here to indulge in sport."

"From the looks of things I'm ideally placed to be behind bars for the rest of my life."

"The possibility is there, but not the inevitability. If you did not kill Harte, Mr Green and I are as anxious as you are that you shouldn't be blamed for it."

"I didn't kill him. Never had any thought of doing the poor old sod any harm. He was a poor bit of a thing. A cripple. Why would I want to kill him? He was the only one round here who showed Maisie and me friendship. We liked him."

"What did you particularly like about him?"

"His voice," said Maisie, softly. "He spoke so nicely. And he was always the same. He never seemed to get down like other people. He was a real tonic to be with."

"His guts," said her husband. "He was only half a man, but he'd got more guts than all the rest of Lowther put together. And he was independent. You had to watch your step and see you didn't try to help him too much."

Green asked: "Did you try? At first, I mean."

"Once. I put a hand under his arm to help him. It was the only time I ever saw him riled."

"Angry?"

"Not loud and cross, like. But the look he gave me! I really wondered what was up."

"He said nothing?"

"Just looked at me as though I was muck. But he was all right the next minute. But I've never tried to help him since."

"I have," said Maisie flatly. "And he never gave me a dirty look."

"There y'are then," said Rencory. "That proves it. He'd got such good manners that if one of the ladies helped him, he'd be polite to her, even though he hated it like hell. But let a gent try his hand and he'd warn him off. And why not if he didn't like it? If he'd not done anything about it he'd have had people helping him like a baby the whole time, and he was too gutsy to want that. I told you he was all guts."

Masters said: "You've given me an admirable picture of him."

"Maybe. But what sort of a picture have you got of me? Slipping him poison?"

Green got to his feet.

"Now listen, matey. You pride yourself on being a hard-headed business man. I'll bet you're always saying you face facts."

"That's right. I do."

"I'll also bet you use your nous, too. Instinct I suppose you call it. If the facts make some deal look good, but your nose can tell it stinks, you throw the facts out of the window and do what your instinct tells you to do. Right?"

"Of course. I've always done business by the seat of my pants. I know my game and I back my hunches."

"Well, we know your game, too. We're looking at facts. But up to now, they don't add up. Otherwise, you'd be in the nick. We're using our nous, too. We're looking for more facts and we're not going to move against you or anybody else until facts and intuition both point in the same direction. So if you're not guilty, forget it. If you are, carry on nail biting. But remember, so far the chips appear to be stacked against you. When your chemist gets here we may get a few more facts that will help you—or convict you—as the case may be."

"You're bloody certain you'll get it right."

"We will, mate. Or at least we won't get it wrong."

"I wish I could be as sure."

Maisie looked across at Masters. "Milton didn't do it, you know."

"I've still got to try to eliminate him, madam. And I can't honestly consider him above suspicion until I'm satisfied how a poison which he possesses in his factory killed a guest in his house. But as Mr Green has said, we're very anxious not to make a mistake, so you can rely on us to do our utmost to place the blame fairly and squarely where it belongs."

And with that she had to be satisfied. Bill Boardman's car drew up a few moments later. Green answered his ring at the door.

Masters guessed the newcomer's age at about thirty-five. As Rencory had said earlier, Boardman was one of those fair young men who always look extremely well washed. Even now, in dusty work shoes, old trousers, open-necked shirt and soiled lab coat—which he had obviously not stopped to take off—he looked clean and wholesome. He gave the appearance of having hurried, even though he had made the journey in a car.

Boardman ignored Masters and made straight for his employer. "What's the trouble, Mr Rencory? Apart from what you told me on the phone this morning?"

"What did Mr Rencory tell you this morning?" asked Masters.

"Just that Mr Harte had died here, apparently of poison, and that the local police had asked him to stay here and not come to the factory today."

"Did Mr Rencory say what poison might have been the cause of Mr Harte's death?"

"Not a hint."

"I told you I didn't know," growled Rencory.

Masters was urbane. "At least Mr Boardman's answer to my question goes some towards substantiating your assertion that you didn't know."

"Thanks. It didn't sound to me as if that was why you were asking."

"What's all the mystery about the poison?" asked Boardman.

"Merely that it's a very little known toxin, Mr Boardman. Ricin, in fact."

Boardman's reaction to the news was similar to that evinced by his employer on learning that ricin came from castor oil seeds. He put his hand to his mouth. "Oh, God in heaven!"

"You, at least, have obviously heard of ricin, Mr Boardman."

"Of course I have. It comes from castor oil seed and we've got a load in stock."

"What are your professional qualifications, Mr Boardman?"

"Mine? Oh, I've got a BSc in Applied Chemistry, Grad RIC in analytical chemistry and HND in chemical engineering."

"So you would know about extracting ricin from castor oil seeds."

"I should hope so. But it doesn't come direct from the seeds themselves."

"No? You mean if I were to eat the seeds I wouldn't poison myself?"

"You would—most likely, if you ate enough of them. But you couldn't eat them by mistake."

"Why not?" asked Green.

"You've obviously never seen one. They're big—anything up to an inch long and half an inch wide. Oval, smooth and shiny and of a most uninviting ash-grey colour."

"They sound just like the kidney beans my old man used to plant on his allotment years ago," rejoined Green, "and I ate those as a nipper."

"Maybe, but these seeds come out of a fruit covered with tough spines . . ."

"Like a conker?"

"Just like a conker. Each fruit is divided into three compartments each containing one seed, and each seed is supposed to resemble a rather nasty insect called a tick . . ."

"Blood suckers?"

"That's right. The latin generic name for the plant is the same as that of the tick."

"Spare us the culture, mate." pleaded Green. "This is complicated enough without that."

"Just as you like. But you'd have to make a great effort to eat the seeds in their original form."

Masters came in again. "You suggested that ricin would have to be processed from the seeds."

"That's right. Shall I explain?"

"Please do."

"Right. The first thing we do in the factory is to express the oil. We pass the seeds through rollers. This cracks the husks off. We seperate these from the kernels by an air blast. Then we press the kernels. You've probably seen the presses, made up of alternate metal plates and filtration pads. The metal squeezes the oil out and the pads filter it so that very little of the gup flows into the vats. But the point is, we do this process cold. And that's very inportant. Hot pressing would be more efficient, but with castor seeds it's not on."

"Please explain why."

"Because above fifty degrees centigrade you stand a chance of dissolving out ricinine, which is a toxic alkaloid. Your ricin poison is a toxic albumin."

"Go on."

"We express three times, usually. Getting diminishing amounts of oil each time. And what we're left with finally is the pomace, or feed cake."

"Which you sell for animal foodstuffs?"

"Not just like that. This is where we use heat. We subject the pomace to steam treatment and this destroys the ricin, making the pomace safe for feed or—sometimes—fertiliser. At the moment, I'm researching a new product especially for cows, using the pomace as a base, together with a decoction from the leaves of the plant. It is to be used as a galacto-gogue—an idea I got after hearing that certain native tribes use poultices of the leaves for local application . . ."

"Here, wait a minute," said Green. "If galacto-gogue means what I think it does . . ."

"Inducing a flow of milk."

"Right. Then these poultices for local application . . . ?"

"For native mothers who had difficulty in breast feeding their babies."

Green shuddered. "And put on scalding hot, I suppose, like my old mum used to use bread and linseed poultices when my knees festered after falling as a kid. It was bloody painful on the kneecaps, but what it would be like on the . . ."

"Mixed company," murmured Masters, "should not be subjected to your childhood memories, however graphic." He turned to Boardman. "We've followed you so far. The ricin is left in the pomace."

"That's my point. It could only be dissolved out of the pomace, not out of the original seeds."

"How would one get it out of the pomace?"

"Simply by graunching the pomace around in water. The albumose . . ."

"Ricin?"

"Sorry, yes. The ricin is soluble in water and neutral in reaction. If you filter the water from the pomace, you've got a solution of ricin. Dry it out fairly slowly in a moderately warm place—on a plate or a saucer, perhaps—and you're eventually left with a little bit of white amorphous powder so actively poisonous that you could knock out half London with a tablespoonful. And I'm not joking. Ricin is no fictional poison. It's a fact—as Harte's death will have shown you."

"How much of this did Mr Rencory know?"

Boardman stared straight at Masters. "Nothing. His knowledge of biological sciences or any other sciences for that matter is non-existent. He's a salesman and administrator. Nothing more."

"But surely he's not an unintelligent man, as his success in business proves. So after years of processing castor oil seeds he ought to know something about the chemistry."

"Who said anything about years? This is the first time we've ever handled castor seeds. It wasn't until we got into this new factory that we could have coped with them. And they came in at my instigation. I wanted to research this new galactogogue, so I ordered them up. All Mr Rencory would have known about them was that they were coming. And only that because he has to approve bulk orders, and he naturally wants to know what research and development is envisaged."

"He had the general picture, but not the details."

"That's right."

"And you've only had one load of castor seeds delivered?"

"Right again. They turn rancid fairly quickly and are then unfit for extracting the oil. As we're only at the research stage, we don't need large continual supplies. We stabilised the whole lot some weeks ago . . ."

"By processing it?"

"Yes. Now we can work with it in our own time without fear of loss."

"You lost some, chum," said Green.

Boardman took this seriously. "Maybe. But I shan't believe so until it has been proved.

Masters said: "We're rushing our fences. Mr Boardman, you say your employer would know nothing of the dangers connected with a pomace of castor oil seeds?"

"That's right, he wouldn't."

"Who is responsible for the safety provisions of the Poisons Acts in your factory?"

"I am."

"Are you asking me to believe that you have dangerous substances such as untreated pomace on your premises without warning all who work there that the material contains a deadly poison?"

Boardman's face fell.

"I'm waiting for an answer, Mr Boardman."

The scientist swallowed. "I did issue warnings," he said at last.

"To everybody?"

Boardman nodded.

"And posted warning notices throughout the factory?"

"Yes."

"So Mr Rencory would be aware of the dangers?"

"I suppose so."

"Why then did you say he would know nothing of them?"

"I meant he would know none of the details—of the chemistry involved in isolating ricin."

"Can I believe that, Mr Boardman? As a scientist you have been trained to be very exact in your use of words. Can you give me any form of guarantee . . . ?"

"Of course I can't. But I've worked with Mr Rencory for seven years. I'm doubtful if he knows the formula for common salt."

"I don't, Mr Boardman, but I could extract ricin from castor pomace right now if there were any here."

"Because I've just told you."

"Quite. One hasn't to be very knowledgeable—if one can learn the simple facts of an experiment such as a young schoolboy could do successfully."

"I suppose not."

"You know not. And I don't doubt that lying about in your office are enough textbooks on pharmacology and articles on this project of yours to give anybody—layman or otherwise—the necessary information to extract ricin from pomace."

No answer was needed. Boardman's face told Masters he had scored an easy bull. "So you are still saying Mr Rencory would have had too little knowledge to arm himself with a pinch of ricin powder or a few drops of solution?"

Boardman flushed to the roots of his fair hair. "I'd swear it. You've asked my opinion, and that's it."

"Thank you for giving us the benefit of your assessment."

"You sound as if you didn't believe me."

"Say slightly sceptical of your opinion. It's not that I think you have uttered any untruths. And I must admit that you, as the professional on the spot, are the one most likely to give me the true picture. But there's one answer you haven't given."

"What's that?"

"If not Mr Rencory, then who?"

Boardman looked about him as though it were

slowly dawning on him that he himself could be a candidate for suspicion. "Who? I don't understand."

"It is almost certain that the ricin originated in Mr Rencory's factory. Mr Rencory's guest died from ricin poisoning, in Mr Rencory's house. Somebody carried the poison from the factory and administered it to Mr Harte. Somebody. Who, Mr Boardman?"

Rencory himself, who had been sitting quietly throughout Boardman's strenuous defence of him, now spoke.

"Nobody from my factory came to this house yesterday."

"Except yourself."

"Well, of course *I* did. It's my home, isn't it?"

Masters considered this for a moment and then said reflectively, as though he had no real interest in what he was suggesting: "There is, of course, the possibility that the ricin came from another source. If that proves to be the case it will be the coincidence of all times, but we must, nevertheless, consider it."

Green grunted. "It's an impossibility. And you know it. I'll bet neither of our cattle cake kings here can name a source within a hundred square miles."

"No nearer than London itself," admitted Boardman.

"And not everybody's importing castor seeds," said Rencory. "At least I hope not. Bill here's in first with galactogogue—or he'd better be. I don't want any market going sour on me just when we've got an expensive launch on our hands."

"I think that disposes of that problem," said Masters.

Maisie Rencory, who had been curled up in a corner of the sofa, her eyes restless and fearful throughout the conversation, fluttered her hands. "Oh, no. You promised to try everything. You must look, just in case."

"In case what, Mrs Rencory?"

"In case somebody else has some castor oil seeds. Mr Boardman has told you Milt couldn't have done it."

Masters went across and sat down beside her as if to give her reassurance against what he was about to say.

"Mrs Rencory, when crimes of this nature are committed, we policemen look for these things. Opportunity, means and motive. Now I've no shred of evidence or suspicion which makes me think that your husband had any motive for killing Roger Harte. But, and it's an important but, motive is the least important of the three. What I mean is, that it is not incumbent on the police to prove motive in a court of law. Opportunity and means however, are different kettles of fish entirely."

She looked up at him. For a moment he thought she was about to slip her hand into his for comfort. Instead, she said: "But this is different. Milt may have had the opportunity and the means, but he didn't have the knowledge."

Masters looked at her gravely. "I agree with what you say, and it is most important. But you are asking me to look two ways at once."

"How?"

"A few minutes ago, Mr Boardman said your husband hadn't sufficient knowledge, and you have just reiterated it, although I have pointed out that very little awareness of the biological or chemical sciences is needed to extract ricin."

"Yes, but . . ."

"Please hear me out. Just as it would be a very great coincidence if there was a second source of castor oil seeds in the vicinity, so it would be a great coincidence if there was a second group of men aware of how to produce ricin also in the vicinity and at the same time inimical to Roger Harte."

"I don't know that I really understand that."

Boardman said: "I don't think you have to, Mrs Rencory. What the Superintendent is saying, in effect, is that the ricin must have come from our factory and it must have been extracted and administered by somebody who had access to it in our factory—in other words, one of us."

Masters held up both hands. "Not quite, Mr Boardman."

"No? You just explained how, for it to be otherwise, you'd have to swallow three dirty great coincidences which even I couldn't bring myself to accept."

"Thank you. But you ended your explanation to Mrs Rencory by a simplifying phrase—'in other-words, one of us'. Now, while I'll agree that the substance of what you said is correct, at no time have I suggested that the person concerned is one of you—whoever 'you' may embrace."

Rencory had been sitting quietly. Masters knew it was costing this bumptious man a great deal in effort not to keep butting in on the conversation. Now, however, he had his say.

"So you lot reckon the stuff came from my factory. You reckon it's on the cards I knew how to process ricin. And there's no doubt about the fact that Roger Harte died here. There's equally no doubt that he'd been here for some time before he died and that he was in normal health when he arrived. What does that add up to?"

Masters got to his feet.

"You tell us, Mr Rencory. In my place what would you do?"

Rencory gazed at him for a long moment.

"I'd arrest me."

Masters continued to stare straight at him.

"And I'd be wrong," continued Rencory, "because I bloody well know that I didn't poison old Rodge, though I can't expect you to believe that."

Masters shrugged his shoulders. "I don't see why not—if it's true. You see, Mr Rencory, I may not be prepared to believe you too readily. But by the same token I'm not prepared to disbelieve you too readily. So that leaves you—for the time being at least—just about where you were. And us. So I shall not arrest you, Mr Rencory, but I should be grateful for your assurance that you will stay in Lowther tonight."

"Of course I'll stay. I'm not the sort to be driven out of my own home by a load of bloody rubbish like this."

"Very stalwart of you, sir. Do make sure you look after your wife, too. This is a very trying time for her. I'm sure you have a suitable bottle to open to have with your supper."

As they left number twenty-seven, Green said: "Do you know what time it is?"

"Judging by the fact that a number of business-type husbands appear to be arriving home after the toil of the long day, I'd say somewhere about six o'clock."

"Right."

"Meaning you think it is time we, too, called a halt for the day."

"Before you make any more generous gestures to suspects, yes I do."

Masters turned to the gate of number twenty-eight. "You think I should have arrested Rencory?"

"At least had him in for questioning."

When they reached their temporary incident room, Masters sat down. "So you think I'm wrong."

"Never let it be said!"

"I'm surprised you think so."

"You reckon I always think you're right?"

"I'm aware you rarely think I'm right. But this time I did think I'd get your approval for holding my hand over Rencory."

"Then you've got another think coming. He'd got opportunity and means. That's enough excuse to start cracking down on him. So why you should think I'd agree with letting him off the hook is beyond me."

Masters put his feet up on the desk.

"If I were to take him in, I have a feeling I'd be playing direct into the hands of the people round here." He looked up. "The people you despise so much. The lotus-eaters of Lowther Turbary."

Green grunted. "They'd all like to see him taken up."

"Quite. But for what reason?"

"Eh?"

"Why should they be pleased to see Rencory detained?"

"They all think he's guilty."

"Ah! Now here's one of my big reasons for not coming out of next door in company with Rencory. If solving a difficult murder case looks so easy that all his neighbours feel they can do it—and all arrive at the same conclusion—I can't help suspecting that they've overlooked something, somewhere, and that they've made a colossal bloomer. Otherwise, teams like ours are unnecessary. All one has to do is take a consensus vote. And I'm not buying that. I happen to take a deal of pride in my work, and consider it a difficult job that few people can do as well as we do it in our own little firm. So I'm not subscribing to either popular desire or popular prejudice, and Rencory stays out of jail until I'm good and satisfied I've got a cast-iron reason for putting him there."

"I knew it wasn't your social conscience working," sneered Green. "It's your pride."

"And my wits," said Masters quietly. "Ah! The sergeants are returning."

They waited in silence till Hill and Brant were with them.

"Get owt?" asked Green, picking his teeth with a matchstick.

"Nothing new," confessed Hill. "We've visited another nine houses and spoken to children, mothers and fathers. It's the same story, from kids and grownups alike. They all thought Harte was an outstanding bloke. They could all cite instances of his little kindnesses and humour. Two women cried . . ."

"Did they now?" asked Green. "Nice bits of stuff, were they? Bints he could have had a bit of hanky panky with at some time?"

Brant stared at him in distaste. "You heard what he was like. He was disabled."

"Makes no difference. A crippled body doesn't mean a crippled appetite."

"There was nothing to suggest they had ever had

any amorous dealings with Harte, Chief," said Hill. "And they were both getting on a bit. I think they were the emotional ones you get in every community."

"Thank you."

"You can get all mardy about it if you like," said Green, unabashed. "But I've said it before, and I'll say it again. There's a woman mixed up in this somewhere. Stands to reason. Poison! So if Roger boy had got a few bits of homework around the Close, well, we'd want to know, wouldn't we?"

Masters got to his feet.

"Coming from the chap who, a minute or two ago, was sneering at me for not arresting a man, I consider that a bit rich."

"I didn't say there wasn't a man in it, too."

"You have a theory?"

"Not what you'd call a theory. But if Rencory also had his eye on a bit of local capurtle that Harte rather fancied . . ."

"Spare us," groaned Hill. "No bit of local capurtle likely to appeal to Harte would look at Rencory. And you know it."

Green sucked a tooth and raised an eyebrow in resigned agreement with the force of this statement.

Chapter VI

Masters sent the other three ahead in the car to The Gleaner. He himself turned into the gateway of number nineteen, the house of Harriet and Leslie Casper, Sally Harte's greatest friends and her temporary hosts.

He'd deliberately left the widow until after the preliminary enquiries had been made. The background material he now possessed meant that the interview would not start cold. He was primed, to some degree, with a feeling for the ambience in which the crime had been committed.

The door was opened by Leslie Casper. It was obvious he had only recently arrived home. He was still in a dark city suit. Masters' first impression was of a handsome man. The genuinely handsome. Not one of the modern, loose-lipped, drug-eyed toughies, nor one of the older matinee idol types. A man with good features, clear-eyed, reasonable length hair greying slightly, a good breadth of shoulder, a hand clasp that was neither bone crushing nor jelly-fish like, and a voice that needed no cachet of status to make it authoritative nor humour to make it kindly.

"You must be Detective Superintendent Masters."

"Word got around, has it?"

"Of course. The Lowther grapevine is the most perfect communications system yet devised by man—or should I say by woman? But apart from that, I would have recognised you. You appear in the press from time to time."

"Notoriety."

"It might be regarded as such in some circles."

"Not in yours?"

"I'm a lawyer. Legal director of a finance house to be more precise. But what are we standing here for? Come in, Mr Masters."

"Thank you. I've called to see . . ."

"Sally Harte. I must say I appreciate the fact that you've left it until after my return before approaching her."

Masters made no disclaimer. If Casper felt that, as a lawyer, he could in some way look after the interests of Mrs Harte, there could be no objection. But if this was so, it did just raise the question of why Casper thought his guest's interests needed to be protected.

"I'd like a talk with her. Shall you be present?"

"You've no objection?"

"None whatever, providing Mrs Harte doesn't mind."

"Sit in here and I'll fetch her. Help yourself to a drink meanwhile."

It was the same room that could be found in every house in Lowther Close. But this one seemed more lived in. Slightly untidy, with bookselves a yard high down one wall, holding several hundreds of assorted titles, by no means all legal tomes or business manuals. A galleried silver drinks tray stood on a small rosewood chest. Carved wooded coasters were laid about as though waiting to accept drink glasses—an open invitation to sit back in the well-worn armchairs and enjoy oneself.

Masters chose gin. He had poured it and was standing in the window by the time Casper rejoined him.

"Sally will be right with us. She's just popped upstairs to put a dab of powder around her eyes."

Masters turned. "She has taken her husband's death very hard?"

"They were very close. Very."

"Some of your neighbours are a little surprised at her reaction."

Casper was helping himself to whisky. "Really? In what way?"

"They say that she is naturally a woman of great self-possession. One who can cope with any and every situation. That she has nursed and cared for a seriously disabled man without allowing it ever to upset her equanimity."

"That's true. Sally certainly stands firm under fire."

"And yet she goes to pieces in the face of a death . . ."

"Her husband's murder."

". . . a death which, though sudden and ill-timed, cannot have found her totally unprepared."

"For her husband being poisoned?"

"For his death—from whatever cause. A seriously crippled man is unlikely to live his full span."

"I see what you're driving at. But I suggest you've got it wrong."

"Please tell me how."

Casper sipped his whisky before replying. "It is because of her care and attention that he lived so long. Without her love he'd have gone under long ago. Probably when he was first injured in '44."

"Are you saying that Mrs Harte nursed her husband through the initial tragedy?"

"She virtually took over after the surgeons had done their bit—say about a fortnight after the incident."

Masters sat down. "Mr Casper, can you tell me what the incident was in which Harte sustained his injuries?"

Casper put his glass down. "I can give you the general picture, but not the details. Roger—to the best of my knowledge—never told anybody the whys and wherefores of that business."

"Not even his wife?"

"Not even Sally."

"Can you say he did not confide in her?"

"No, but I've often speculated about it."

"With what conclusions?"

"That the incident was so harrowing he thought it would upset her. Cause her unnecessary pain."

"You must have some reason for being so definite—apart from the fact that Harte was a kind man who would never wish to hurt anybody, let alone his wife."

"I have. From what little I know of it, the whole business was an unnecessary tragedy. It wasn't even caused by enemy action. What happened was this . . ."

Casper got no further. They could hear the voices of two women talking as they came downstairs. Mrs Casper and Mrs Harte were on their way to join them.

"I shall be in The Gleaner this evening," murmured Masters. Casper replied with a nod as the two woman entered.

As he was introduced to her, Masters mentally classified Sarah Harte as a strong woman. Strong in character. Strong in body. As a young woman she would have been handsome, with an attractiveness of face and figure which would have been best set off by the sophistication of simple clothes—probably even severe ones. Now her hair was greying, but her brow was clear and her eyes, slightly puffed from weeping, glittered with intelligent awareness. Her dress was of white piqué, with navy blue belt and collar. No hint of mourning. Her legs were bare; still strong and well shaped. Her sandals blue and white.

Masters murmured a few words of condolence and felt, as he did so, that they were being weighed, syllable by syllable, to test their sincerity. He guessed they were accepted as platitudinous and felt slightly annoyed that though he was by now too accustomed to murder to react greatly, yet his revulsion at violent crime had in no way diminished, and so his sympathy—even when uttered routinely—was never less than genuine.

"You wish to ask me some questions, I understand."

"If you please, ma'am."

"I should like to be present," said Casper. "As a solicitor and friend . . ."

"I have no objection," said Masters mildly. "So long as you don't mind, Mrs Harte."

Sarah Harte didn't mind. She gave the impression of preferring a gallery. So much so that she asked Harriet Casper to stay, too. Masters raised no objection.

They covered the ground already reconnoitred by

DI Woodside. Sarah had left for London in time to be in Piccadilly for lunch at one. In the afternoon she and her friends had attended a fashion show and had tea. Thereafter they had taken an early dinner and attended a theatre. She had returned by train.

"Were you expecting your husband to meet you at the station, ma'am?"

"No. I had left the car there for the day. Roger never drove."

"Never? I mean, there are cars which can be adapted . . ."

"My husband always said he preferred to be driven by me than to have what he always referred to as a motorised bath chair."

"If Sarah wasn't available," said Casper, "Roger would never have had any difficulty in getting a lift anywhere. I myself usually drove the four of us in my car if we went out together for the evening. Everybody in Lowther would have helped out—at any time."

"I see. You left his supper ready prepared for him, Mrs Harte?"

"Not exactly."

"Please explain."

"Because I never knew, if I was away from home, where Roger would eat. He could drop in anywhere and get a feed. And that is what he often did even if I'd left him a properly prepared meal. So I told Roger before he left home yesterday morning that should he decide to eat at home, he would find a tin of breast of chicken in the refrigerator. I didn't open it because it dries out if left too long out of the tin."

"Anything else?"

"For the reasons I've already explained to you, I felt I wouldn't leave a salad prepared either. And in any case, Roger wasn't very keen on lettuce. A small tin of asparagus tips was more to his liking. The two tins would be as much as he would eat in this weather."

"No potatoes?"

"He rarely ate them. He had a horror of getting fat because he could take no strenuous exercise to keep him in trim. He'd have an Energen roll and soft margarine if he wanted anything with the chicken and asparagus."

"And no sweet?"

"If he wanted more he'd have biscuits and cheese. But I doubt whether he would have touched them last night. His appetite was fairly small."

Harriet Casper said: "Roger would often make a meal off just one item that tickled his fancy. Only last week when we were out to dinner together he ordered a steak with nothing before, with or after it. He got by on it, too, where others of us never would."

"Thank you. That helps me a lot."

"It means," said Casper, "that any poison he may have ingested could not have been in the food he ate in his own home."

"It certainly seems so," said Masters, making a mental note to ask the pathologist to confirm the contents of the stomach. "So now we have that problem out of the way, can we suggest a reason, Mrs Harte, why your husband should have visited Mr and Mrs Rencory immediately after his supper?"

"Before we come to that," said Sarah, "I think you are puzzled as to why I should leave tinned food for a man with a crippled arm to open. The answer is that we have an electric tin-opener which a baby could use—as doubtless you have seen in your examination of my house."

"I have been nowhere in your house except Mr Harte's study, ma'am. Nor have the other members of my team. And I should like to add that I have heard so much about how well you looked after your husband, that I would not have the impertinence to question the food you left him, or its form."

"I apologise for what must have sounded like rudeness. But you were puzzled about something. I could see it on your face."

"I was wondering why you hadn't made definite alternative arrangements for his evening meal. The Gleaner keeps a decent table."

"You mean I should have made arrangements other than those my husband requested?"

"You mean he actually asked to be left a meal at home?"

"Yes."

"I would have thought that such a request indicated that he intended to work at home last evening."

"That is how I read it."

"And yet he went straight to visit Mr and Mrs Rencory. Can you offer any explanation for that?"

"None. Other that that he must have changed his mind."

"Did he often change his mind?"

"Never," said Leslie Casper. "Roger was iron-willed. Velvet covered, of course. But once he'd decided his course of action, nothing altered it."

Masters looked at Harriet Casper. "Is that how you saw Mr Harte, ma'am?"

"Very much so. There are countless instances of it.

Why, only three weeks ago over the business of the disco at the tennis club . . ."

"Don't bother Mr Masters with our parochial affairs, darling," said her husband.

"Please," smiled Masters. "I'd like to know."

Encouraged, Mrs Casper told her story.

"Roger said the club should do more for young people. He said we were losing too many of them because we were fuddy-duddy. We hold a social evening every Saturday night in the summer. But there was a lot of opposition from the old and bold to introducing barbecues instead of bridge, and as for a disco! You can guess what some of them had to say to that suggestion. But Roger wouldn't be put off. Old Mrs Mayhew who's years over sixty was the leader of the antis. She went on and on about the noise levels and what she termed loose behaviour and so on. Roger told her that she and her friends should attend to see there were no immoral goings-on, and he personally would look after the noise.

"And he brought it off. All the old pussies turned up, certain that there would be a rumpus."

"But there wasn't?"

"Of course not. The DJ Roger had hired came with all his loudspeakers and things. He tested them and found they were loud enough to shake down the club hut, and then went off to get a drink. Roger was a very clever electronics man, you know. As soon as the DJ's back was turned, Roger did something to the amplifier. When the shindig started, the DJ was at a loss to know what had happened to about a hundred of his decibels, and he wasn't clever enough to find the fault and put it right. So we had a comparatively quiet, orderly couple of hours. Then Roger went round persuading the older people to leave. As soon as he'd seen a mollified Mrs Mayhew—and her cronies—off the premises, he sent the DJ off to have a break. That's when he put the amplifier right. After the interval, with the old squares away, the kids had a good noisy disco. Everybody was satisfied. But it shows Roger would never be put off. Difficulties in his way were only there to be overcome. He knew what he wanted to do and he did it. And he never did anything without a good reason—but please, remember, the accent was always on the good."

"Thank you, ma'am. I can take it, then, that you would imagine Mr Harte knew exactly what he wanted to do last evening?"

"You can. I think he intended to visit the Rencorys."

"Without telling Mrs Harte?"

Harriet Casper shrugged.

"He wouldn't tell me that," said Sarah. "He'd know I wouldn't have approved."

"No?"

"I detest that uncouth man and everything about him."

Masters paused a moment before going on. "But you used to visit Mrs Rencory yourself, and she you."

Sarah Harte blushed. "That was different. Where he was an uncouth bully, she was a mouse, a nonentity who needed friendship and company. I merely offered it as a neighbour."

"And you can think of no reason to cause your husband to plan a visit there?"

"Plan?"

"I thought we had agreed that your husband did little without a purpose. And you say he did *ask* you to leave him that sort of supper ready."

"My husband, for some reason best known to himself, was cultivating Milton Rencory."

"Just as you were Maisie Rencory?"

"If you say so."

"Shall we say that is the way it appears to an outsider. A kindly man making a friendly gesture to a disliked man. Had Mr Harte not asked his neighbours to treat Rencory with courtesy and friendship?"

"He certainly had," said Casper. "He'd asked everybody to be decent to him."

"And from what you told me about him, Mr Harte would have been successful."

"Eventually, yes, I suppose he would, to some extent. Mark you, even Roger would have found it tough going."

"With you and Mrs Casper for instance?"

"Ugh! I told Roger he was putting his friendship with us—and others like us—to a severe test by asking us to accept Rencory. He just isn't our type."

"Did he know Mr Harte was pleading his cause in the Close?"

"Of course he did."

"Then, as a lawyer, you would say it was extremely unlikely that Rencory would poison his own champion?"

"I refuse to answer that beyond saying that I have no difficulty in believing anything unreasonable of Rencory."

"Quite right," said Harriet Casper. "He has an ungovernable temper. I thought he was going to strike me one day when Switch—that's our little Cairn terrier—wet his gate post."

"Mr Harte was not struck down in a fit of rage. Poison suggests long-calculated murder. Very few people—in my experience—have hasty tempers and cool calculating minds."

"Maybe not," said Casper. "But Roger died in Rencory's house. From what poison, I don't know. But he'd been in there for some hours when he died. Most poisons act pretty quickly."

Masters got to his feet. He had more to ask, but felt the time was not yet. He'd prefer to sort out what he already had before proceeding further.

As Leslie Casper saw him out of the house, Masters asked: "You will be at The Gleaner tonight, won't you?"

"About nine o'clock."

"Thank you. You couldn't make it now, could you? Before your supper?"

"I don't see why not. Hang on, I'll just tell Harriet."

Green was in the bar. Masters went across to him.

"Come and meet Harte's best friend, Leslie Casper."

"That him?"

"He's going to tell me what he knows about how Harte was crippled."

"The tank accident Rencory mentioned?"

"I assume that's it. I'd like you to hear. You've already got some bee in your bonnet about it, haven't you?"

"Yeah! Nothing certain. But my memory's stirring."

"I'll get the drinks. Stay and help me carry them over."

There was no more than half a dozen people in the bar, but Casper had chosen a table close to the window and taken a seat on the upholstered wall settle.

He had opted for gin. Masters and Green were drinking Worthington.

"Detective Inspector Green, Mr Leslie Casper."

Green put down the beer to shake hands.

"Mr Casper is a solicitor as well as being a close friend of the late Mr Harte and Mrs Harte."

Green grimaced. "How's it feel to have your best pal murdered?"

Casper was a little surprised by this bluntness. He made no reply. But Green made no allowance for the niceties of conversation as practised in Lowther. "We reckon that one of your immediate buddies knocked him off."

"Impossible! Nobody in Lowther, except . . ."

"I know. Except Rencory you were going to say. And he's no buddy of yours."

Casper raised his glass. "I find the situation totally confusing. On two counts. First because I cannot imagine how anybody as thoroughly decent as Roger Harte can become a candidate for murder; and second, how anybody in our mutual circle could kill a man—whoever he was. Therefore, I suggest that whoever poisoned Roger did not know him, and that means that the killer is not resident in either Lowther Turbary or the Close."

"It's a viewpoint we haven't lost sight of," said Masters. "In fact, we wish to widen our enquiries now. That is why I should like you to tell us what you know about how Harte received his injuries. So far we have been told it was a tank accident. I know very little about tanks, but I should have thought that an accident with one was a strange thing to happen, unless Harte fell under it. And if that happened, I'm surprised he got away so lightly."

"Quite right," said Green. "He still had his limbs. If he'd gone under one, the tracks would have nipped his arm and leg off like clippers paring finger nails."

Casper put his glass down.

"What I have to tell you is not only hearsay, it has been gathered together bit by bit over the years. And that means that some of it may even be the work of my imagination."

"Never mind, let's have it," said Green. "I've heard stories that sounded at first as if they came from a blathering granny when her belly's full of buttermilk, but they've helped. Your pal Harte was a pretty unlucky sort of chap . . ."

"Unlucky? How do you make that out?"

"He came out of the last struggle looking something like a lump of raw beef that had been chopped up by a buzz saw. That ruins his life. Then he gets himself murdered. That stops his life. Me, I believe there's often a connection between bits of scabby luck like that."

"You're playing hunches."

"Why not? We've only been here eight hours. Nobody's left us much in the way of material clues on the scene. Fingerprints aren't going to help, or fag ends. Or even poison containers, because there aren't any. It's all in the mind, this one, Mr Casper."

"I see. So it's background information you're seeking."

"That's it," said Masters. "And so, as a solicitor, and therefore an officer of the court, you need have no qualms about repeating hearsay, Mr Caspar. I'll just top up your drink and then you can begin to tell us how Harte was injured."

* * *

Casper began slowly.

"Harte, as you probably know, was a gifted young man. He was outstanding academically as his career since the war proves. He was also extraordinarily good at games, as his double blue shows. He took his degree—first class, by the way—in 1940, after we had been at war less than a year. He wanted to join the RAF, but as he had slight astigmatism, he could not be considered as a pilot. So, because he had been a member of the OTC at school and university and had gained Certs A and B, he joined his county regiment."

"Did he go overseas?" asked Green.

"Not until after D-Day in '44. In the meantime he had been commissioned and had met and married Sally. As you can guess, Sally was the type of girl who was hell-bent on doing her bit. Like so many girls of her type she was completely untrained for any class of war work. Nevertheless she offered her services in any capacity, but said she preferred to become a nurse if possible. It so happened that at the time she volunteered there was no acute shortage of nurses, but there was a desperate need for hospital dispensers. Phamacists in those days were usually male, and all those young enough were being called up into the RAMC and the like in the other services for work in field ambulances and sick bays on ships and aerodromes. The base hospitals were hardest hit, so it was decided to run crash courses for intelligent young women, to teach them how to dispense medicines.

"Sally was one of them. She was working in a hospital just outside Lincoln when she met Roger. They were married in April 1944, with ten days leave for a honeymoon and then, in May, all leave and travel was cancelled because of the preparations for the invasion.

"So they had just ten days together as man and wife—with Roger as a fit man, that is. He went over to France with an independent brigade in June. In August he was brought back a mangled wreck and taken to a hospital in Tidworth to die. Sarah got an immediate compassionate posting down there. She did her work and nursed her husband at the same time. The authorities put him in a small, private ward and she slept there, in a camp bed, beside him. When the war ended he was just getting on to his feet. Sally had given him the will and the strength to live after the doctors had virtually thrown in their hands." Casper sipped his drink. "So now you know something of the bond between those two. And it probably explains why a cool, self-controlled woman like Sally should break down when her husband is murdered."

Affected emotionally, Green slurped about a quarter of a pint of Worthington to hide his embarrassment. Masters gravely filled and lit his pipe before another word was spoken.

"Can you tell us anything of the accident itself?"

"I know it happened on August Bank Holiday Monday. Not that anybody out there was aware that in peace time it would have been a holiday, but Roger remembered. He was like that. Remembered little things that others missed. It was just before the rout of the Germans at Falaise. The enemy was holding on to Pinçon like grim death to allow his troops who were dropping back in front of the American sweep, to hinge into a line parallel to the Seine, presumably as preparation for an orderly withdrawal northwards. It didn't happen, of course, but Jerry really was scrapping like billy-ho at that point. On this particular day, Roger's brigade had been pushed into the line just there. His battalion was centred round a French farm which the enemy was mortaring mercilessly. The companies away from the farm weren't getting quite as much stick as HQ Company."

"And I suppose Harte was in HQ Company," said Green.

"Specialist platoon commander. He'd got his chaps well spread out a bit to the front of the house. He himself, with his runner and signaller, was using the absent farmer's air raid shelter. That wasn't quite as safe a billet as it sounds. It was simply a hole in the ground, well away from the house and covered with a few planks, an old bedstead and about a foot of earth.

"The mortaring was growing heavier and causing casualties. But that particular brigade had no artillery of its own for blasting the enemy positions."

"They had to rely on Army Group to assign Gunners to them," said Green. "And they weren't always as fast moving as some of the regular divisional units."

"The artillery assigned to Roger's battalion was decidedly slow in showing up that day, apparently. The officer who was going to observe for the battery didn't arrive at the farm until half past three in the afternoon. He drove up in a tank for a briefing from the infantry CO. His arrival called down even more enemy fire, I understand. At any rate, Roger remembered hearing this tank arrive and looked out, hoping it was a whole squadron prepared to go forward and silence the mortars. He was sadly disappointed to see just one Gunner officer get out of the turret with his mapboard and run over to where the CO was waiting in the farmhouse."

"If he'd had much experience," said Green, "Harte would have realised that, once they got weaving, those guns would have done what he was wanting just as well as, if not better and quicker, than a handful of tanks."

"Maybe. Anyhow, after what I imagine to have been about ten minutes, Roger heard the tank start up again and it headed straight towards them in their covered trench."

"My god!"

Casper nodded. "As I understand it, Roger was on his way out to wave the tank away when it hit them. The officer had got inside and closed his turret flaps because of the mortaring, so he didn't see where he was going and couldn't have been guiding his driver."

"The bastard!" breathed Green. "Moving among troops on the ground when closed down! I suppose the driver was closed down, too, and just using his periscope which doesn't give a view of the ground in front of him."

"I can't say. All I know is that the tank hit the trench longways and half toppled in. The other two occupants were killed, broken by metal bed irons forced into their bodies by the weight of the tank. Roger, half out and half in was . . . well, I suppose you'd call it crushed, all down his left side from his temple to his toes."

"It must be true," said Green. "It must be. No body could think up anything . . . hey! Wait a minute! What happened to the tank and its crew?"

"Nothing. I believe they were unaware of what they had done. They went on about their business.

All the other soldiers were cowering under cover, and it was some time before anybody realised that Roger and his companions had been hurt."

"And the tank commander got away scot-free?"

"Apparently. The stretcher bearers who collected Roger knew nothing of the incident. I suppose the casualties were reported to the adjutant who took it for granted they were caused by the mortaring. In any case, everything was in a state of flux and our own people put in an attack with more tanks and infantry through that position soon afterwards. So who was to say which tank had been responsible in the heat of battle?"

"Incredible," murmured Masters.

Green was sitting silent and angry.

"Did Mr Harte ever tell you who the tank commander was?"

"Never. I doubt if he knew."

"Thank you for telling us this, Mr Casper. As DI Green has said, I doubt whether you imagined much of the account you gave us. It seems so right."

Casper nodded. Masters signalled to the barman for refills. Green drained his pint pot noisily in preparation.

As they sat down to dinner, Hill said: "We've been round all the most obvious spots, Chief. The village shop, post office, fruiterer's and garage."

"Nothing new?"

"Not much. He was well known and well liked, but he didn't have much to do with any of them."

"He wouldn't, would he?" asked Green. "A bloke like him doesn't fetch the groceries, and he didn't drive the car so he wouldn't go near the garage, except as a passenger."

"True—but false," said Hill.

"Funny you should mention the garage," said Brant. "That's the one place he did go to occasionally. For bits and pieces for his workshop."

"What sort of bits and pieces?"

"I dunno! Bolts, I suppose. Oil for his tools, perhaps. Oh, yes. He once bought three twelve-volt car batteries. Second-hand ones from wrecks. Still in going order, of course. Used them in his electronic experiments, or so the proprietor said."

Green grunted and the conversation lapsed. Masters seemed disinclined to talk, and Hill, accustomed by now to his moods, guessed that the Chief had gone broody, as he always did when a tricky one began to show signs of piecing together.

Hill was surprised at this. As yet he could see no reason why the case should break. He looked at Brant. His colleague, looking up from the slice of melon he was eating, raised his eyebrows. So Brant, too, was aware of the signs. Only Green appeared oblivious. He was taking tomato soup strangely quietly for him, and consulting a wine list.

As he finished his soup he pushed away his plate and said bluntly to Masters: "It was Rencory in that tank."

Masters paused before replying. "It would seem so. From what Casper said, Harte saw him running between the tank and the farmhouse. Would he recognise him again after nearly thirty years?"

"Anybody would recognise that mug. But why shouldn't he know the name?"

"I don't know. You tell me."

"There's no reason why not. They weren't kept secret, you know. And Harte was in HQ Company. He'd always be around when the Gunners called in for an orders group or a drink. There was close liaison between OP officers and the troops they were supporting. If Rencory had been in support or attached on a previous occasion . . ."

"Was that likely?"

"They had no Gunners of their own. They had to rely on AGRA. It was a habit to let the same people work together whenever possible."

"Thank you. We'll assume Harte knew the name."

"You reckon he confronted Rencory with it and threatened to expose him, so Rencory finished him off?"

Masters shook his head. "Nothing so simple. But what a coincidence! Or was it?"

"What?"

"That they should meet as neighbours, thirty years later."

"Not on your flippin'," grated Green. "Not in this part of the world. And in any case, I'll bet a bob Rencory didn't recognise Harte. I'll bet he never knew him."

"But you just said . . ."

"I know what I said. But remember that a Gunner was one man going among a lot of infantry officers. They'd all know him, but he'd not know all of them. Only the CO, second-in-command, adjutant and Company commanders."

"I see."

Masters refused potatoes and started to eat. The

wine waiter filled his glass without him noticing. He ate and drank abstractedly.

Hill murmured "Aye, aye," to Brant, and Green picked a strand of meat from between two teeth.

Chapter VII

When they rose from the table, Masters said to Green: "I'd like you to confirm it for me."

"Oh, yes? At this time of night?"

"It's not yet nine o'clock and it's broad daylight."

"It's bloody hot, and while you stay here supping ale, you want me to traipse around running errands."

"We shall all be working," said Masters wearily. His every impulse was to blast Green for impertinence, but not with The Gleaner's customers within hearing distance. The trouble with Green was that he was always a nuisance, whether for putting obstacles in the way of every suggestion, opposing requests, or simply stinking out the inside of the car by sucking cough drops.

On several occasions, Masters had tried to get rid of Green. Having him along on every important case was like trying to run while carrying two buckets of sand. But the powers-that-be at the Yard wouldn't wear it. Even when Green himself had asked for a transfer to one of the Divisions because he loathed Masters and hated working with him, the answer was the same. The successful quartet was not to be broken up. Because of this official attitude, the sergeants were suffering. Hill, at least, was in line for promotion he had not received in the interests of keeping a successful team intact. Masters had been toying for some time with the idea of forcing authority's hand by bringing matters to boiling point through the simple expedient of staging the long overdue, flaming row with Green. But he had held his hand out of distaste for slanging matches at Green's level—and anything less would not have penetrated. Green was impervious to verbal shafts of wit, sarcasm or cynicism. The blunt instrument was needed, but Masters was not prepared to wield it.

"I suppose you want me to call that bloke, Rencory."

"Not at first. Please go to your Mrs Stockwell, Mrs Summerbee and Mrs Weeks-Baine. Ask them all the same question."

"What question?"

Masters told him.

"Is that all?" Green indignant now.

"Then go to Rencory. Armed with what you know, you ought to be able to confirm what we suspect."

Green glared at him for a moment and then, apparently, the penny dropped. "Come to think of it, I'd like another word with Rencory."

"Keep it to yourself for an hour or two. If, after that, you'd like a man-to-man chat with him, that'll be your own business."

"Too true it will. I've changed my mind about the people in this borough. They'd every right to try and kick Rencory out. After I'm finished with him I reckon he'll be glad to go. An' that's saying something, because I never thought I'd find myself siding with the bourgeoisie."

"We'll walk with you. The sergeants and I will be in Harte's house. Join us there when you've finished."

As they entered Harte's study, Hill asked what Masters wanted them to do.

"Search the house and workshop. I'm looking for the presence—or absence—of certain items." He listed them, explained their significance and sent them off.

He himself remained in the study. He went to the bookcase built into the alcove beside the fireplace. Technical books, mostly. Some biographies and a novel or two. He searched the shelves and at last found a volume he thought might be interesting. He was reading it when Hill returned to the room.

"No batteries in the workshop, Chief. I looked round pretty well without disturbing anything. I reckon I found the corner where they stood, though. It's a concrete floor. Some of the acid must have spilled out and attacked the lime in the cement. It's pitted."

"I suppose you can't tell when they were moved?"

"Oh, yes, sir. Pretty recently, I'd say. At any rate, the rectangular marks are there—ridges of dust and metal filings—the usual sort of things you'd get in a shop that hadn't been swept after you've moved something that had been there for a bit."

"You turned the bonfire over?"

"Yes, Chief. You were right. I've got two chunks in a bag."

"Thank you." Masters went on reading for a few

more minutes and then put the book away, just as Brant joined them.

"It's been dismantled, Chief, but some of the bits are up there in the spare room among the luggage and other junk."

"What, exactly?"

"It's difficult to say just how it was done, but there's a trembler coil with spring-loaded points."

"How would it work?"

"Off a car battery, sir, you use the coil to get a higher HT voltage. The primary LT circuit collapses and is induced into HT current in the secondary windings. As you know, in a car, this results in a great stepping up from the original twelve volts to many thousands—high voltage, low current. And if this is working without being suppressed, the effect can be disastrous to a TV or radio at least a hundred yards—if there's no form of screening."

"Would he be able to work such a device without upsetting every set in Lowther?"

"I think so, sir. He could screen it with metal: just a piece bent round with a small opening pointing in the direction he wanted, or he could have pinned a lead into the aerial cable or something he, being an electronics expert, would know about and I don't."

"Thank you. I'd like a look at the workshop, now."

Hill asked why, as he himself had just examined it.

Masters didn't answer. He led the way through the house, both sergeants accompanying him. Harte's workbench was just as the dead man had left it the last time he had been out there. Masters examined the shaped pieces of metal, each clearly labelled with magic marker. Using long-nosed pliers to hold them, he picked up two strips barely two inches long and a quarter wide. One had three tiny studs braised on it. The other had three holes. He put the two together. They matched: married. He admired the workmanship and stood thoughtful for a moment.

"Look after these, Brant. Prime evidence. I want them tested."

"What for, sir? Prints?"

"Traces of ricin. Bag them for the forensic lab."

He returned to the house. As he reached the front hall, Green arrived. "You're right. Dead jammy."

"Good. Did you get the tube?"

Green opened his hand to display what it contained.

Masters nodded and led the way into the study. There he slowly filled a pipe and lit it. When it was going to his satisfaction, he turned to Hill.

"Get Dick Woodside on the phone. Tell him I'd like him here as soon as possible."

Green asked: "You're going to leave it to him? The arrest?" He sounded glum.

"I think not, this time."

"Why not?" asked Brant. "You usually leave it to the locals."

"Shall I tell him to bring a warrant?" asked Hill.

"If he wants to make the arrest himself tonight, he can have one of our ready-use ones."

"You can't leave it to him," insisted Green.

"I've said I'd rather not."

"He's friendly with all these people. It wouldn't be right to let him take one of them up on a murder charge."

Masters didn't reply. He looked out of the window. It was after ten o'clock but the last of the daylight still lingered in the Close. Lights were coming on in houses. Windows were open and curtains drawn wide. There was the sound of music from a radio: a burst of happy laughter: the soft hum of a motor car.

Green was right. He wouldn't allow Woodside to make the arrest. The friendship angle would be sufficient excuse. He could plead that it was because Woodside might be emotionally involved that he himself had been called in. So even though he normally left local arrests to the local police, he would change his habits this time. Not willingly, of course, because he knew that to make the arrest gave the locals a sense of being in at the kill and of not being entirely left out in the cold by the interlopers from the Yard. And there was the point, too, that arrests such as this gave him—Masters—personal mental hell. So often his sympathies had lain with the murderer rather than the victim ...

He pulled his thought up short.

"You're right. We'll have to do it. Tonight. See that Brant gets that tube to send to forensic."

"DI Woodside is at his home, Chief. They're passing a message telling him to come here."

"Thank you. Hill, I want some beer. Bottles of it. Take the car to The Gleaner. Get a dozen—no fifteen, if Woodside is joining us. Three each should just about see us through this session. Oh, and tell the landlord we shall be late, so if he'd like to give you a key ..."

"Right, Chief."

After Hill had gone, Green said: "You're mighty sure of yourself."

"Don't you agree with me?"

"You can leave me out of this. I'm only guessing at who we're talking about, and I'm not entirely sold."

"Oh?"

Green nodded towards Brant. "Do these two know?"

Brant glanced from one to the other. Green answered the implied query. "You know he's all set to make an arrest. Guess who?"

"Haven't the faintest."

Green turned to Masters. "There you are, you see. If you want me to buy it you'll have to do some explaining."

"When Dick Woodside comes, and the beer. I don't want to go through it all twice."

Green grunted, pulled out a new packet of Kensitas and the bag of cough lozenges. He was about to pop one of these in his mouth when he stayed his hand. "Better not. It'll only spoil the beer." He lit a cigarette instead and handed Brant the tube. "Bag this up, too, Sonny Jim. Taken from Rencory's house ten minutes ago."

Hill was back with the beer and five glasses before Woodside arrived.

They were helping themselves to drink when the DI came in, mouthing a question. "What's gone wrong? Something that couldn't wait till morning?"

"Nothing's wrong."

"Then why the urgent message?"

"I thought you would like to know the results of our investigation at the first possible moment."

Woodside stared open-mouthed. "You mean you've finished, sir?"

"That's right. The arrest can be made as soon as I've explained."

"Who is it?"

"Patience, lady," said Green. "We don't just blurt

out our secrets. We give you a report—verbal to begin with, just for your personal benefit. Written, later, for official purposes."

"I see."

"Sit down, Mr Woodside," said Masters, "and help yourself to beer. Fortify yourself, in fact, because I imagine some of what you are going to hear will be a bit of a shock to you."

"Like what, for instance, sir?"

Masters threw the reply away phlegmatically, thereby enhancing the effect of the few quietly spoken words.

"Oh, just that your saintly Roger Harte was planning to murder Rencory."

The beer Woodside was pouring went unheeded over the side of the glass. Even Green snorted in disbelief, while the two sergeants, wiser than Green, set their glasses down simultaneously, registering surprise like a double act on the halls.

"Say that again, sir."

"You're spilling good beer."

"That about Harte murdering Rencory."

Hill was the first to recover from the shock. He turned to Masters. "You murmured something earlier about whom God wishes to destroy he first drives mad. Then you went on to say something about there being no god but Harte."

Masters grinned with satisfaction. "Smart of you. Harte was the little tin god of Lowther—albeit a pleasant, benevolent sort of god."

"How do you square that with your statement that he intended to murder Rencory, sir?"

"I'll tell you. Harte was a man of great determination, probably stubbornness. I think we can safely claim that, because his whole life since the war has been a determined fight to overcome injuries which would have put other men into wheelchairs. But over and above that, we have been given other instances in his everyday life—such as when he determined to hold his disco evenings despite much opposition from club members and went to a deal of trouble to ensure they were accepted. Remember that he achieved it, not by charm of manner, but by a rather devious method which envolved using his professional knowledge of electronics."

"How does this show he was going to kill Rencory?" asked Green.

"We know that the injuries which ruined the life of an extremely able young man need never have happened. We even think they were caused because a certain man in a tank was too frightened for his own skin to look where he was going."

"We're dead right about that," grunted Green. "I've just had a word or two on that subject with Rencory."

"Oh yes?"

"He denies his head was down because of the enemy mortars. He said the infantry CO had given him all the map references from a one-inch map and as he was using a one over twenty-five thou, he had to convert them and mark his own map up pretty quickly. Said the job was urgent and he couldn't do it standing stuck up in the turret like a spare you-know-what."

"Is it a likely explanation?"

"Could be. Sounds authentic. The infantry never used as large a scale as the Gunners. No point. They didn't need to know much about the country more

than a few hundred yards in front of their rifle bar-
rels—and they could see most of that with their own
eyes."

"Whichever is the right answer, Rencory maimed
Harte. Obviously Rencory didn't know the identity of
the man he had injured or indeed, if we are being
charitable, can we say for certain that he knew he
had hurt anybody. I imagine that going over one
hump in a tank is much the same as going over any
other. But I think it fair to assume that Harte knew
Rencory's identity."

"He can't have done," objected Woodside. "Or if
he did, he never told anybody round here. The news
would have spread like wildfire and I'd have got to
hear."

"We are told by Harte's friends of long standing,
and even by his wife, that he never mentioned the
name of the man responsible. Rencory isn't the com-
monest of patronymics, so had Harte ever mentioned
it, it would have been called to mind quite readily
once a neighbour bearing that name moved into the
Close. But DI Green assures me, from his knowledge
of the relationship which commonly existed between
infantry and the observing officers of their supporting
artillery units that Harte would most definitely know
of Rencory by name and sight. Whether it was one or
the other or both is immaterial, because we have
Rencory's evidence—with no reason for him to falsify
it—that Harte, on his visits to Rencory's house, often
discussed his host's wartime experiences, but seldom
his own. I submit that this was Harte making sure beyond all doubt that Milton Rencory, the neighbour
was, in fact, the Gunner observer who ran over that

trench in a French farmyard on August Bank Holiday Monday, 1944."

"Good point," conceded Green. "That bit about Harte making sure."

"I get the impression he was that sort of man. Thorough."

"No!" groaned Woodside. "Not thorough at murder."

"Thorough—so as not to make any mistake over the identy of his victim," insisted Masters. "The act of a basically decent man who intends rough justice."

Hill interrupted. "I've followed everything so far. And I agree with it. But I've not heard anything which sounds like real evidence that he was planning rough justice."

"No?"

"No," said Woodside. "Roger Harte was the one person round here who showed Rencory any kindness. Why should he do that if he intended to kill him?"

"Perhaps because, had he done so, he would have hoped to hear the local DI—yourself—take just that point of view."

"Christ! You can make anything fit."

"Can I? Do I? As the local inspector, hasn't it occurred to you that in the very short time he has been here, Rencory has been involved in too many bizarre events for them to be just everyday happenings or coincidences? Take that postcard from the debt collector to begin with. That was bogus. Fixed, in other words, to discomfit Rencory. You said so yourself. First, who had the most reason to hate Rencory?"

"From what you say, Harte."

"Second, name me somebody else in the Close, other than Harte, who would send that card."

"There's nobody I can think of."

"Third, who else was involved besides Rencory?"

"I don't get you."

"Who received the card first?"

"Harte. But the postman . . ."

"Yes. The postman. But forget him. He was only wanted to spread the story. Who took the card to its ultimate destination to witness Rencory's discomfiture?"

"Harte."

"Quite. I needn't go on with that particular incident. But consider a few of the others we've heard about today. The snowstorm on the new TV set, for instance. The garden fire that ruined a hundred pounds' worth of new paintwork. The rumpus over closing the path to the tennis club."

"What about them?"

"They all concern Rencory. But there's another common factor. Harte."

"Oh, yes?"

"Television set first. A snowstorm on a brand new, expensive set, just at the moment Rencory wanted to watch his favourite programme."

"That's life."

"Not in this case. It was death. I imagine that if ever a man was likely to die from blood pressure or apoplexy at that moment, it was Rencory. Fortunately, he doesn't take things lying down. He set out to find what infernal machine was causing the interference. Who was it got up from a friend's dinner table to help him?"

"Harte. And it shows what a good chap Roger was."

"A bit discourteous to his hostess, wouldn't you say?"

"Well . . . a bit out of character, perhaps?"

"Look, Dick," said Masters. "Harte went to Rencory's house, switched off the set and removed the back. Then charging Rencory strictly not to switch on in his absence, he came into this house—his own—on the pretext of getting some tools. He went back with a screwdriver or two, tinkered for a moment or so, replaced the back, switched on and hey presto! the picture was perfect. What had Harte done?"

"Mended or adjusted the set."

"He'd come in here and switched off a powerful, unsuppressed make-and-break appliance which he'd rigged up in his box room and started up before leaving the house. He'd probably screened it so that it was strictly directional for Rencory's benefit."

"How do you know?"

"Sergeant Brant found it, dismantled, this evening."

"But why?"

"To drive Rencory mad," said Green. "You heard."

Woodside shook his head in bewilderment.

"This afternoon, DI Green interviewed Mrs Hermione Stockwell who told him a story about how Rencory's garden rubbish heap mysteriously caught fire while Rencory and his wife were absent from their home."

"He could have lit it before he went out, and it smouldered for some time before bursting into flame. I looked into that fire . . ."

"But not far enough, Dick. Mrs Stockwell described

the soot and smoke that was coming off very exactly. She said there was heavy, dense smoke with clouds of unburnt particles coming from it. But there wasn't the sulphurous smell of burnt oil."

"I remember."

"She mentioned rubber and—significantly—chlorine."

"I thought Rencory had probably chucked an old motor tyre on the heap."

"Did you turn it over to check?"

"Of course not."

"Well, I'll tell you a little story. When I first joined the force, a few years ago, now, I was assigned to a case concerning a mysterious outbreak of gas poisoning and some deaths in a whole area of the East End. Of course, I was very much one of the lesser lights in that enquiry, but I can recall that it took a little time to unravel. What we eventually discovered was that some bright spiv had bought up for next to nothing a whole heap of army surplus batteries. He'd seen his opportunity because coal was short and it was still the mains of heating in most areas. After salvaging the plates, he'd cut up the battery cases with a circular saw. The chunks looked not unlike coal. He'd hawked them round by the sackload, selling them as fuel. And they did burn—there's no denying that. And in house fireplaces, the chimneys took away most of the heavy smoke . . ."

"Probably accounted for all those killer smogs," grunted Green.

"Very likely. But a lot of the fumes escaped into rooms and gassed whole families. With some fatalities. Chlorine gas, Dick. The stuff they used in the first war."

"And you reckon this is what Mrs Stockwell smelt?"

"I'm sure of it. Battery cases are made of a form of rubberised plastic, very dense. When they burn, they give off heavy hydrocarbons and unburnt particles."

"So Rencory had an old battery on his fire and not a worn-out tyre."

"Wrong again, Dick. Go to your local garage proprietor and ask who it was bought four or five old batteries from him."

"Harte?"

"Yes. Then look around this house and the workshop and see whether you can find those batteries."

"They're missing?"

"We know where they are—or what's left of them. Some charred remains under Rencory's garden fire heap and a couple of pieces in one of our forensic specimen bags."

Woodside was bemused. "What . . ." he began. "What put you on to this?"

"DI Green reported Mrs Stockwell as saying that though the garden fire had obviously been going for some time, Harte had declared he hadn't noticed it."

"That's quite likely, if he was in here and absorbed in what he was doing."

Masters inclined his head as if to acknowledge the possibility. Then he continued.

"Mrs Stockwell said that when she and her husband returned home they found Harte standing by the fire holding the end of a hosepipe that had no flow of water through it."

"He hadn't had time to turn the tap on."

"Come off it," grunted Green. "Just think what you would do if you wanted to put out fire a bit smartish. You'd fix the hose to the tap and turn it on and then

get down there to squatter the water and to hell with
anything else. Harte was an intensely practical man.
He'd do things the best way—which in this case meant
the quickest. He was also a cripple. Yet he'd clam-
bered through a hedge once with his hosepipe. Are
you going to say that that was just to lay it out, and
that he proposed to buffet his way through that
hedge twice more—first to go an' turn on the tap and
second to get back to play at firemen? Rubbish, mate.
He was out there staging a 'what-a-good-boy-am-I'
stunt for the Stockwells' benefit, but he took damned
good care not to dowse the fire he'd started."

"But why should he do that? Why?"

Masters stretched his legs. "To put Rencory in bad
with his neighbours—part of the psychological process
of driving him mad."

Woodside shook his head. "This sort of investigation is beyond me. I'm all right with tangible facts,
but not with this sort of mental probing you go in
for."

"Then it's time you began," said Masters grittily.
"And if we're talking about facts that stare us in the
face, what about the closing of the path to the tennis
club?"

"What about it?"

"You heard of it?"

"Yes. My wife and kids sometimes used it when the
Nicols lived there."

"Think, man," urged Masters. "Nicol was president
of the club so it was understandable he wouldn't
mind his neighbours using his garden as a right of
way to the club. Rencory, however, was not a tennis
buff, so it was understandable he should stop trespass
on his property. But Harte—he was the secretary of

the club, and his garden offered just as good an access to the courts. So why didn't he open up when Rencory closed down?"

"I don't know. It probably didn't occur to him."

"The answer to that is extremely short and rude. It occurred to DI Green and to me within minutes of hearing the story. Harte was a man not short on grey matter."

"True enough."

"I suggest that it was just another of his ways of causing the name of Rencory to become a hissing in Lowther. With a long-term effect. Because you see, Dick, every time a member had a long walk to the club, he would curse Rencory. But if a new way had been opened up, the fact that Rencory had closed his down would be forgotten—with no rancour to keep it in the forefront of people's minds. And that is what I think you, as the local DI, should have been aware of. And had you appreciated it, you might have become suspicious about all the other troublesome events round here which concerned Rencory and yet had Roger Harte as a common factor."

Woodside's face reddened. "Are you saying, sir, that I could have prevented this murder."

"It would be foolish to suggest that. But I am pointing out that prevention of crime is a policeman's prime job, and if we don't apply our minds to accepting hints, we're not going to be very successful. And I believe that this tragedy is to some extent a case in point in that nobody realised that Harte was pulling the wool over everybody's eyes by pretending to befriend Rencory while hating his guts to the extent of planning his murder."

Green snapped his fingers excitedly. "That's it.

Remember what Rencory said about when he went to help Harte out of a chair? He said the look Harte gave him was enough to kill. Yet Harte allowed Maisie to help him without turning a hair. Rencory put it down to the fact that Harte hated being helped by anybody, but always acted like a gent with the ladies."

Masters nodded.

"How was he going to murder Rencory?" asked Woodside belligerently.

Masters shrugged. "I don't know. I doubt if he's written the plan up as he did for his artificial heart. But I have no doubt whatsoever that one of these bright days Rencory would have picked up something that would have given him an awful shock."

Woodside's face still registered disbelief. Masters smiled at him. "Come on now. I told you to fortify yourself against a very strange story. I haven't really begun yet."

Green lit a fag. "Hardly," he said. "So far all he's got from you is the fact that a bloke who was planning murder got the chop himself. But you haven't told him who was wielding the axe."

"I thought it would be good for DI Woodside to hear what he has so far been told—just as background material, of course, for what is to come."

"There's more in the same vein?" asked Woodside.

Masters nodded. Hill said: "I don't know why anybody's sceptical about what we've heard so far. I notice nobody's picked any holes in the Chief's reasoning. So what about it, Mr Woodside?"

"I knew Harte. You lot didn't."

"The onlooker sees most of the game, sir."

"If we're going to start bandying that sort of old

saw about, Sergeant, I'll remind you that the leopard doesn't change its spots."

"Nobody is suggesting that Harte changed at all," claimed Hill. "As I understood the Chief—reading between the lines, like—I'd say Harte took a vow on August Bank Monday thirty years ago to get Rencory."

"For maiming him?"

"Probably. Although I reckon it would suit your book better if we agreed that it was to avenge the two soldiers who were with him and who were killed by Rencory's tank."

"By the left!" breathed Woodside. "I never looked at it that way. Now I can see . . ."

"Well done, Hill," said Masters. "I must confess I'd been thinking of personal revenge. You'll see why, later. However, whatever the reason, I believe Harte had decided to kill Rencory. Not that it was an implacable intention. What I mean is, I don't think he would have ever deliberately set out to track Rencory down. But I think his feelings could best be summed up in what is really a quite common phrase, even if not always meant to be taken literally. Some phrase such as: 'If ever I see that bastard again I'll kill him'. Many of us say such things and don't mean them. However, Harte being Harte, and a very determined man, meant it."

"How can you possibly know that?" asked Woodside.

"Because, laddie," said Green, "he never once, in all these years, mentioned the name of the man who crippled him and killed his soldiers. Now you just think about that. If it hadda been you or me, we'd yelled our heads off, shouting his name and demanding our pound of flesh. But not Harte. And why not?

It was because he knew that if ever he breathed the name Rencory and then the opportunity to kill him arose, he'd be an automatic suspect. In short, what I'm saying is, that Harte knew that once he breathed the name, it was as good as a free pardon for Rencory. And however kind Harte was, he wasn't prepared to let pal Milton off the hook that easily."

Woodside poured himself more beer.

"OK. So let's suppose I agree with you. Where's it getting us?"

"I'll push on," said Masters. "DI Green was quite right in saying that Harte never mentioned Rencory's name over the past thirty years. Consciously, that is. But let me remind you of what Jenny Summerbee told me. She overheard a conversation in which Harte replied to his wife who had said: 'You haven't been sleeping well lately'—and these are the important words—'No? Don't tell me I've been talking again.'"

"Talking in his sleep," breathed Brant. "Of course. Old thingummybob—you know, Chief, the trick cyclist—he gave us those lectures at the Yard last year. I remember him saying that you start to talk in your sleep when emotions rise to the surface. He said it meant that the conscious was taken over by the unconscious, and this happened usually when there was some great tension or emotional upset to trigger it off."

"Gawd! The stuff they teach young coppers nowadays," groaned Green. "The psychology of crime!"

"Nevertheless, he's quite right," said Masters. "I think the near presence of Rencory and the intention to murder him brought Harte's emotions to the surface and caused him to talk in his sleep."

"There'd only be his missus to hear him," said Woodside.

"Quite. But just recently wasn't the first time she'd heard him talk in his sleep."

"He did say 'again', didn't he?" murmured Brant.

"Yes, he did. And when can we assume the first time was?"

"Got it," said Green. "Old Casper said she'd been allowed to sleep on a camp bed in his room in the military hospital when he was brought home from France. I'll bet his emotions were centered on Rencory then all right. I'll bet she heard him spill the beans then."

"That's right. I think that is when she got to know that her young, gifted, handsome husband had been almost crushed to death unnecessarily by an unthinking lout. Probably she didn't get Rencory's name. It could have been that she wasn't concerned with who had caused the damage. Not then. My guess is she was totally immersed in nursing her husband back to life. But what a life! Instead of a marriage of glorious youth, her lot was to become nursemaid to an impotent cripple. That was her portion for the last thirty years. No children, no physical love from the man who, when she first married him, was by all accounts as fine a physical specimen as any woman could rejoice in and look forward to consorting with for the rest of her life. This, I submit, gentlemen, made Sarah Harte a very bitter woman."

"No!" said Woodside. "She wasn't."

"Not to other people, perhaps. But can you believe that any woman, robbed of what she was robbed of, knowing the cause to have been totally unnecessary, was not going to bear some grudge against the person responsible?"

"Put like that . . ."

"Thank you. I do put it like that. Over the years the bitterness must have mounted and then, through her husband's ramblings in his sleep, she learns that the man who had done this terrible thing to her had moved in next door. A loud-mouthed, self-satisfied, uncouth man, and this creature had been the instrument by which her happiness and that of her husband had been curtailed. How do you think she must have felt?"

"Like murder, I suppose."

"And that is just what she set out to do—murder. Whether on her own account or to avenge her husband, I don't know. But I incline to the former, because I don't think many people commit murder on behalf of others—without payment, that is. That is why I made the remark I did when Sergeant Hill suggested that Harte was planning murder on behalf of his dead soldiers."

"Are you trying to tell me," asked Woodside, "that both Roger and Sarah Harte were planning to kill Rencory?"

"Yes. And separately. Unbeknown to each other. It is my belief that Roger Harte had no inkling that his wife was planning murder; and by the same token, I believe that she only entered the arena because she thought her husband was not planning to kill Rencory."

"This," said Green, "takes the cheesecake biscuit. I've met collusion between husband and wife murderers, but I've never before heard of a married couple planning separately, at the same time, to kill the same victim."

"I believe it only happened because Roger Harte was too successful in his pretence of befriending Rencory. Even his wife misread his actions and thought her husband had gone soft. So she stepped in without saying a word to him . . ."

"Why not?" asked Hill. "Apparently she was used to doing most of his chores for him. So why not murder?"

Woodside snorted and got to his feet. "This has gone far enough, sir. This joke. I've not fallen for it. But it's getting late now and time to call it a day."

"Siddown," ordered Green.

Woodside paid no attention. "I shall report to my superiors in the morning and suggest that the Chief Constable takes the case out of your hands."

"As to that," said Masters, "I shall be off the case tomorrow morning. I shall be handing it over to your superiors as signed, sealed and delivered. And we're not playing a practical joke on you just because you had a run-in with one of our number this morning. So be a good chap. Help yourself to more beer, sit down and listen."

Woodside looked around him. Brant got up, opened a bottle and handed it to him. Finally he sat down, slowly.

"You'll be telling me next that Sarah Harte killed her own husband."

"Quite right. That's exactly what happened."

"You're learning, laddie," said Green.

"She did it inadvertently, of course," said Masters.

"I give in, sir."

"Not completely, I hope, because before we're finished we shall have some of those tangible, material facts you seem to prefer to the sort of nuance we dredge up."

"Thank heaven for that, because if I were to explain this to my Chief Super . . ."

"You won't have to. It'll be written down, in full, in the report."

Masters got to his feet and crossed to the bookcase. As he did so he said to Woodside: "Do you know what Sarah Harte did in the war?"

"No, sir. I never heard, and quite frankly I never gave it a thought, beyond the fact that she was Roger's wife."

"She was a trained hospital dispenser. Not a pharmacist. A dispenser. Somebody who made up medicines under a pharmacist's overall authority."

Woodside frowned. "You mean she'd know about the effects of poisons and drugs?"

"A little. Not all that much. Some of it she would have to know. A little more would brush off. But as a dispenser her chief job was the practical one of filling prescriptions in the forms most suitable for ingestion by the various patients."

"Meaning what, Chief?" asked Hill.

"Meaning that in those days there weren't so many ready prepared dosage forms as there are today. Chemists and dispensers had to be able to mix potions in the right proportions, roll pills, make tablets, beat up ointments, grind ingredients with a pestle and mortar and so on and so on."

"Got it, Chief."

"Mrs Harte was taught this art." He took the book he had consulted earlier from the bookshelf. "Here is one of her bibles. It is the RAMC textbook of pharmaceutics. Here, on page 930, is a section entitled: 'Moulded Tablets or Tablet Triturates.' I'll paraphrase it for you by way of explanation."

"We're all ears," grunted Green, striking a match on his shoe sole.

"Good. Here goes. Moulded tablets are small ones composed of the active ingredient diluted with lactose or dextrose and made by a process of moulding . . ."

"You don't say!"

". . . after moistening the dry ingredients with a liquid made up of equal parts of alcohol and water. Just enough of the liquid to make a pasty mass.

"Now here's an interesting bit for you, Dick. The mould consists of two parts. An upper perforated plate and a lower plate having projecting pegs that correspond in position to the holes in the upper plate, and which fit accurately into them when the upper plate is superimposed on the lower one."

"I get it," said Woodside. "You work the paste you were talking about into the holes of the upper plate, smoothing off both sides so that the material is flush with both surfaces."

"Quite right. The upper plate is then placed over the lower one and the contents of the holes are forced out by the pegs. So on each peg you are left with a small tablet which you lift off and dry."

"How?"

"According to this, drying between forty-five and sixty degrees is recommended. I presume that means centigrade, although it doesn't say so, but it does say that drying in air is discouraged because air-dried tablets retain sufficient moisture to support fungal growth, etcetera, etcetera . . . so that means a low oven, in cookery terms. It adds that the higher the proportion of alcohol added, the harder are the tablets . . ."

He shut the book and handed it to Brant for retention.

"She could have used her ordinary oven," said Hill with a shudder.

"Never mind the oven," said Woodside, "what about this tablet machine? She couldn't have one of those around the house."

"But she had. A miniature one. Her husband made it."

"You just said he didn't know what she was up to."

"He didn't. Brant, show Mr Woodside the pieces of metal we took from the workshop."

Brant handed them across, still in their plastic bag. "Part of the mechanical heart," said Masters. "Don't take them out of the bag. Forensic's going to find traces of ricin on them, we hope. There's enough room to fit them together . . ." He watched while Woodside married the two beautifully machined pieces. "Like a glove, isn't it?"

The bag was passed back to Brant.

"Tangible evidence for you at last," said Masters with a grin. "And before you ask the obvious question about what the tablets were made of, think about the size of the holes in that plate. They are, in fact, three millimetres in diameter. Very, very small for a medicine tablet . . ."

"But about the size of a saccharin sweetener," finished Woodside.

"Bravo. Now for what the tablets were made of. Cast your minds back to what we know about ricin and pomace and so forth.

"After the expression of the oil from castor oil

seeds, we are left with pomace. Rencory's people treat this with steam to destroy any poisonous substance which may remain. They then filter it to wash impurities away. This is possible because ricin is soluble in water and neutral in reaction. But if somebody were to steal an eggcupful of pomace . . ."

"Mrs H, for instance?" suggested Brant.

"Why not? She agreed to go round the factory, and according to Bill Boardman she was most interested and paid him a lot of attention. Now, when I heard that, I found it surprising."

"Why?" demanded Woodside. "She is an intelligent woman."

"You must agree, Dick, she's not the sort to relish going round a smelly feedcake factory—particularly one that belongs to arch-enemy Rencory."

"I suppose not."

"You mean she went there intending to pinch a dollop of this pomace, Chief?" asked Hill.

"I rather think that would be too uncertain—to count on finding untreated pomace—but she could be certain of getting hold of a few of the beans and processing them herself. The report I read before we set out this morning said that as few as three have produced fatal results in an adult. They're quite big for beans, but not so big that anybody couldn't palm a score or so when passing an open sack."

"But you reckon she pinched some pomace."

"I do. It was there for the taking. I imagine she went prepared. A plastic bag and an old spoon. Distract Boardman's attention for a few seconds at the critical moment. 'Oh, do go and tell my husband we must get away in time for me to buy a loaf on the way home before the shops shut.' That sort of thing."

"Too easy by half," said Green.

"Isn't it? She'd know about ricin, or had only to read it up in one of her books. She'd also know that they processed castor oil seeds at the factory. It must have come in one conversation or another. I'll bet Rencory is always shooting off his mouth about what he handles or how much the price of seeds has gone up . . ."

"Even I knew he extracted castor oil," said Woodside. "He gave some to Roger Harte for his machinery. The value of castor oil exceeds that of any other known oil, you know. That's why it's used in racing cars. Roger was very happy to use it, he told me."

"That answers that one," said Green. "Anybody got a fag?"

"So," continued Masters, "she got the pomace ready made or made it herself by crushing the seeds. Starting from there, what had she to do?"

"Use her electric mixer," said Green. "The bit that chivvies oranges into juice and makes breadcrumbs and so on."

"Right. She put the pomace in the liquidiser with enough water to wash out the ricin. As DI Green so aptly put it, she chivvied this around for a few minutes and then she filtered it, collecting the liquid and throwing the solid stuff away.

"We know that ricin dries out as a white amorphous powder, so all she had to do was to put the liquid on a saucer and let it dry out—probably in the airing cupboard. So she then had the active ingredient for her tablets.

"All she needed then was alcohol—probably vodka—lactose, dextrose or sucrose or even—and I'm pretty sure I'm right here—she could powder down a few of the pure sweetener tablets themselves, mix the ricin with this powder, and then reconstitute the tablets."

"It would save her going to a chemist's shop to get glucose or dextrose," said Hill.

"Good point. So she made a tablet or two. Not many. She wouldn't need more than one, and she wouldn't have all that much ricin."

"Then what?" asked Woodside, who was by now eager to learn everything there was to be known.

"Before she set out on this course she knew that Rencory used sweeteners in hot drinks—presumably on account of his weight—and that his wife, as we saw this afternoon, does not take any form of sweetener in hot drinks. Coffee and tea, both without sugar, so she was never likely to use one of her husband's tablets. We learned that Mrs Harte visited Mrs Rencory quite often. Kitchen visits, I suppose you could call them. The type of drop-in calls that women on very friendly terms often make."

"It surprised me when I heard that," said Green. "Our gal, Sal, isn't the sort of dame to make a bosom pal out of little Maisie Rencory. Official first visit as required by the etti-ketty books, and after that, nothing—unless, of course, she had some ulterior motive, like slipping a poisoned tablet into somebody's tube of saccharin."

"Is that really what she did?" asked Woodside in amazement.

"Don't sound so flabbergasted, laddie. She probably did it days, if not weeks, ago—when Maisie wasn't looking. It was a clever enough scheme."

"That's true enough," said Masters. "Put one tablet

in among a hundred others, shake the tube, and nobody knows when the lethal one will pop out. Or where. Rencory might have put the tube in his pocket and taken the ricin in his office, or on a sales trip on the Continent hundreds of miles away from Lowther."

"It was bloody irresponsible," exploded Woodside. "She could have killed anybody. Literally anybody."

"She did. She killed her old man," said Green.

"Actually," said Masters, "though the plan misfired sadly from her point of view, I think most people would regard these tablets as quite personal. Not so personal as a toothbrush, perhaps, but the addicts usually carry their own supplies. They're not offered round like packets of fags . . ."

"They were obviously offered to Harte."

"Because he was on his best behaviour."

"I don't get it."

"DI Green got the story not long before you joined us."

"What happened?"

"Harte was a man who took sugar. He bowled into the Rencory's last night just in time for coffee. Mrs Rencory had already brought in the tray. Two cups and saucers, coffee percolator, cream, and sweeteners for her husband. No sugar, because she never used it. Harte appeared, was invited to join them and said he would like a cup of coffee. Mrs Rencory filled the two cups, one for her husband and one for Harte. She then went back to her kitchen to get a third cup for herself. But because it was for herself, and she is not a sugar taker, she forgot to take the sugar bowl into the sitting room for Harte. She rejoined the men, poured her own coffee, and then remembered that

Harte took sugar. She is a nervous little woman. She jumped to her feet again with an exclamation of annoyance at her own forgetfulness. 'There now, I've gone and forgotten the sugar.' 'Not to worry,' says Harte, the perfect gent. 'Don't run out to the kitchen again on my account. Stay where you are. I'll make do with a couple of old Milton's sweeteners.' 'Will you really?' 'Of course, my dear, why not? They won't poison me, will they?' 'Oh, no. Milton takes them all the time.' 'There we are, then. Here, Milton, shove over the tablets, there's a good chap.'"

"That's how it was," agreed Green. "Plop, plop, into the coffee. Stir up. Drink. 'Not bad! Not bad at all! I must get some of these tablets to help keep my weight down.'"

Woodside shook his head. "You people . . ." he began. "How you can . . . do you really think he said 'they won't poison me, will they?' I mean, it's so gruesome . . ."

"Poetic licence," said Masters with a grin. "Just to add a touch of verisimilitude."

Woodside grimaced. "And an hour or two later, Roger Harte was dead."

"Right."

"I've got some more questions."

"Fire away."

"Couldn't that tablet have broken, being bashed about in a tube among scores of others?"

"It could. But why should it? The sweeteners don't break. And remember the book says the greater the percentage of alcohol to water in the mixing, the harder the resulting tablet. Sarah Harte was a dispenser. She wouldn't have overlooked that."

"Wouldn't some of the ricin have rubbed off on to the other tablets?"

"Maybe. Just traces. But not enough to worry about. Actually we are hoping the forensic people can find traces—probably on the inside of the tube or in the dust at the bottom."

"She may have put two in," said Brant. "There could be a second one in there."

"Perhaps, but I don't think so."

"Why not?" asked Woodside. "How can you be so sure?"

"Because that would give the game away too easily. A second person would die in circumstances similar to the first, and should that happen, even stupid policemen like us might begin to get ideas."

"You mean to say you think Sarah Harte thought she would defeat us—you—and get away with it?"

"Did you ever know a murderer—or murderess—who *didn't* think they could beat us coppers?" asked Green.

"I suppose not."

"I'm sure she would try to make it as difficult as possible for us," said Masters. "If she had put two tablets in the tube she would know that the chances of Rencory getting the two of them at once were so slight as to be discounted. So there would be one left to kill another person as I've already suggested, or to give the game away to any policeman who did think to have the tube and its contents examined, merely as a matter of routine. Maybe those she made were flat in both sides where the commercial ones are slightly convex. Or the colour might have been ever so slightly different. Not enough in either case to catch the eye of somebody just casually shaking out a couple to drop into a cup of coffee. But probably enough to be apparent on closer inspection. So I believe there'd only be one poison tablet in the tube."

Woodside suddenly sat up straight as a thought struck him.

"What's biting you, Dick?"

"You said she would make two or three tablets."

"I think she would have to—if only because she'd have to have that amount of material for working up. Her machine would make three. She probably filled all three holes."

"Then there are still some sculling around here, loose. They could be dangerous."

"She probably dropped 'em down the nearest drain," said Green. "I'll bet she got rid of all the residue of that pomace very carefully, too. Days ago. You'll never trace that."

Woodside frowned. "What do you want me to do now?"

"Mrs Harte has to be arrested."

"Tonight? Or tomorrow morning?"

"If you prefer to arrest her yourself, the choice is up to you."

"You want me to take her in?"

"I usually prefer the locals to do it. It saves us a lot of time and bother and it keeps crime within its parochial boundaries. But I must tell you that DI Green has suggested that as you were personally acquainted with both Harte and his wife, it would be a little unfair to ask you to make the arrest."

Woodside looked unhappy. "I'd rather not do it . . ."

"In that case, we will oblige."

"When?"

"If it's got to be done, then it's best to do it at the earliest opportunity."

Hill rose to his feet. "It's after one o'clock, Chief."

Masters nodded. He glanced across at Green who stared at him for a moment and then looked away.

Brant was driving as the Yard car pulled out of Lowther the next morning. Green yawned widely as they left the houses behind.

"Not enough sleep?" asked Hill.

"What do you reckon? Or does two hours keep you going forty-eight hours?"

"No, it doesn't. But I can complain. You can't."

"Oh? Now what bright idea have you got into your crust?"

"You and the Chief. You asked for it."

Green selected a rather bent Kensitas. "You're talking cock, sarn't."

"No I'm not. DI Woodside couldn't see it, but Sergeant Brant and I had you two sussed all the way along."

"Get it off your chest," said Masters, "if you must show how clever you are."

"All right. You, Chief, were as honest as the day is long, explaining that Mrs Harte would have to have made several tablets."

"I was quite right."

"But you didn't say she would keep them in her handbag. And the DI here talked Dick Woodside into believing she'd dropped them down a sink."

"Only a suggestion," said Green.

"Wrapped up in a lot of truth about her getting rid of that pomace stuff after she'd processed it."

"So?"

"Then between you you arrange to make the arrest yourselves. You rarely make arrests, you two. But this time, with a big show of reluctance, you get Woodside to agree because it would have been a painful job for him."

"Are you faulting us on that account?" asked Masters.

"I'm not faulting you anywhere. You stage-managed it perfectly. But we wanted you to know we could see through what you were aiming at."

"That should be good for your soul."

"It is," said Brant. "That bit about if she's got to be arrested it is best to do it straight away!"

"Do you deny the truth of that?"

"No, Chief. But Sergeant Hill told you it was after one o'clock in the morning. You'd made sure our meeting with Woodside lasted late."

"Are you accusing me of discussing irrelevancies in order to waste time?"

"Not irrelevancies, Chief," said Hill, "but you went into minute details which could have been left till later."

"That great goop Woodside had to be convinced," said Green. "You heard him. He tried to shoot down everything we said. He had to be taught his ABC."

"OK. But you two knew that as soon as you hammered on Casper's door at half past one in the morning, everybody in that house would realise what you had come for."

"Really? Casper and his wife knew that we had come for Mrs Harte?"

"Maybe not those two. But Sarah Harte knew. She probably wasn't even asleep when you arrived. As soon as she heard your voices she couldn't help but guess. We don't go around knocking up respectable people in the small hours unless it's for something important. People with guilty consciences don't have to guess why. They know. And you knew Mrs Harte would have kept those other tablets in case of accident."

"How could we possibly have known that?"

"Good heavens, Chief! She was an intelligent woman. She'd want a reserve in case the first lot didn't kill Rencory for some reason. In case he lost the tube; or he poisoned his coffee but before he could drink it he was called to the phone and it was eventually thrown away cold and untasted. And you knew that after last night she would hang on to them. I'll bet she regarded Rencory as responsible for her husband's murder last night, simply for offering him the sweeteners. So he was still for the chop—but more so, if she got away with it. And, of course, she might just have foreseen, right from the start, that she personally might have a need for them in the way she actually used them early this morning."

"Please go on. This is fascinating."

"Is it? You knock on the door, making sure everybody in the house is awake. Then you ask in a loud voice for Mrs Harte. Of course she heard you—as you intended she should. You wanted her to take those pills. Why, we didn't even go upstairs ourselves to get her. You waited for Mrs Casper to come down and asked *her* to go and fetch Mrs Harte—to see she got dressed and packed a case. You gave her time, Chief—deliberately—to take a thousand pills."

"Why didn't you mention all this before we went for her? You might have prevented her suicide."

Hill turned as fully in his seat as possible. "I'm not

blaming you and the DI, Chief. Her suicide was the best thing that could have happened. Life imprisonment for a woman like her would have been bad enough if she'd been convicted of killing Rencory. But for her to be sent down for years for killing her husband—the bloke she loved so much she was willing to commit murder on account of it—well, that would have been worse than anything I could describe."

"What you're saying is that she has paid the price in the most merciful way possible."

"That's it, Chief. I think she wanted to die just the way he did. And I take my hat off to you, Chief, for making it possible. For giving her the choice."

Green stubbed out his cigarette. "Then what the hell are you making all the fuss about?"

Hill stared at him. "You! Complaining about only getting two hours sleep. You aid and abet the Chief in an act like that and then bum your chat because she took an hour or so to die and it kept you out of your bed."

Green yawned widely, and while he had his mouth fully open, popped in a cough lozenge. He then lay back in his nearside corner and closed his eyes.

Masters looked at Hill.

"Forget it, Sergeant."

SOLO

by **JACK HIGGINS**

author of The Eagle Has Landed

The pursuit of a brilliant concert pianist/master assassin brings this racing thriller to a shattering climax in compelling Higgins' fashion.

A Dell Book $2.95   (18165-8)